A Thousand Miles
From Nowhere

by

Larry Farmer

A Thousand Miles From Nowhere
COPYRIGHT © 2018 by Larry Lee Farmer

The Kerr Construction Company COPYRIGHT 2014
Rendezvous with Fay COPYRIGHT 2018

The Wild Rose Press, Inc.
PO Box 708
Adams Basin, NY 14410-0708
Visit us at www.thewildrosepress.com

Publishing History
First Vintage Rose Print Edition, 2018
PRINT ISBN 978-1-5092-2417-3

Published in the United States of America

Dedication

To Charles, Jericho, and Austin,
And to my dear friend Eva Gysi Lash

The Kerr Construction Company

I was surprised how much I liked New Mexico. Being from rural Texas, I didn't have prejudice against hicks and hick places like I pictured were in New Mexico, back before I first traveled there in the summer of 1977. Still I expected to see a bunch of nothing and open spaces. The open spaces were there, but even the desert was beautiful. The land of enchantment. By God, it was true. At almost every turn, behind every hill, red cliff, or mountain, I somehow anticipated buffalo, with Indians on horseback chasing them through the patches of brush and shrubs.

But I still had to get a job.

Gallup was Navajo country. Located off Route 66. The Indian capital of America, they called it, though only a third of the town was Navajo. And it was one of the few places in America that had a sizable Japanese population during World War II that stood up to the Federal Government and didn't allow internment.

I'd heard all my life about Indians and firewater. It was depressing to see sidewalk after sidewalk with at least one drunken body passed out on it. So what was I doing here looking for work? My part of Texas was the poorest in America, the one part of Texas, not coincidentally, without oil. But that wasn't why I was here. I wanted something different. This was different.

****

"So you're Mister Dalhart McIlhenny from Texas." The man wearing a khaki shirt and pants, and a welding cap, sat behind a wooden desk, reading over my application. "Says you're six foot three and two hundred pounds. And you got blond hair with blue eyes. Boy, you should be looking for a job as a Storm Trooper, if you ask me. We got us a long, tall Texan." He laughed, exposing tobacco-tainted teeth. His appearance was gruff, with grease stains all over his clothes, and a slight pudge hanging over his leather belt. "You have a college degree," he said, surprised.

"Yes, sir. I just graduated."

"We don't have any managerial jobs, you know. Old Man Kerr owns this outfit, and he's got three mean sons to help him manage it, if that's what they do. And we contract out our drilling to wildcatters. We have a field foreman, too. All we got is openings for laborers."

"That's what I want."

He scoped me out. "All right," he said, scowling. "Whatever suits you."

He read some more. "It says here you went to Texas A&M," he commented in disbelief. "I worked the oilfields with Aggies. That's what you call yourself, right? Aggies? I spent three years in Odessa in the Permian Basin. One of the most productive oilfields in the world. Seemed like Aggies ran that place. Son, I'm not trying to be condescending, but this doesn't make a lick of sense."

I gave a slight shrug as my reply. He returned to my application.

"Says you were in the Marines. His sons will like that. New meat. You'll see what I mean." He looked up from my application again, even more in disbelief. "You grew up on a farm?" He shook his head and snickered. "I thought people went to college to get away from this kind of life. When can you start?"

"Right now."

"Those steel-toed boots you got on?" he asked.

"No, sir."

"Stop with that 'sir' crap, will you? I work for a living. You'll have to get work gloves, goggles, and steel-toed boots. We'll supply the hard hat. Those are new jeans. You got any old ones? But that's up to you. You can get this stuff at the hardware store downtown. You didn't give an address."

"I just got in. I don't have a place. I have an old van. I can stay in that."

"You mean that old panel truck outside, with 'Desperado' on the side? Is that a Buddha statue on your dashboard?"

I had to laugh. It embarrassed even me. "I didn't want to sleep in my car. I left it back home. It's too small. So I bought the panel truck from a friend of mine just before I left."

"Son, do you have any money?"

"Enough to buy these supplies. Enough to eat on."

"It's minimum wage."

"I know that. I can live on three bucks an hour. I used to work at a cotton gin for below minimum wage."

"And now you got a college degree and are ready for the big bucks. You ain't running from the law?"

"I know it doesn't make sense." I smiled.

"If you ain't running from the law, it's none of my business what you're doing here. Go get your supplies and come on back. The crew's already in the field. I'll take you out there and introduce you. We're doing landscape maintenance on a Navajo reservation. Moriah Energy is strip mining for uranium, and by law they're obliged to replenish the earth. We're contracted by them to make the reservation look normal again. Whatever that means. Environmentalists came in handy for a change. Thank you, President Carter, I guess, for once."

****

The ride to the reservation passed through desolate countryside. I'd heard how sheep and goats can live on the sparsest terrain, and that probably explained why they were about the only living creatures I saw.

The highway was narrow but at least paved. I don't know if everything got suddenly uglier or if it was my attitude, now that I was in the middle of nowhere trying to work for nothing at some menial task. But I remembered, from history class, how time after time the conquered native Indian population was forced on to the worst of the livable and least productive environments.

Our family farm near Harlingen, where I grew up in the southern tip of Texas, an area called the Rio Grande Valley, was irrigated, with good black, fertile soil. We even had citrus orchards. We hired help for below minimum wage, and illegal aliens were even cheaper. Now it was my turn to be one of the hands like we used to hire. I liked the idea. I'd always admired our helpers. *Another reason I'm doing this. I think.*

"Doug." The man who'd just hired me called to a young, husky, medium-height guy with a short cropped beard, after we pulled up to a double-cab pickup. "I hired this guy for your dad. He'll work as a laborer. He just finished college and needs some extra bucks. He grew up on a farm in Texas and is an ex-Marine."

Nothing fazed Doug until that last description of

me—ex-Marine. His eyes narrowed, and I wasn't sure if it was a cynical grin or a sneer on his face. He spit tobacco onto the ground right in front of my new steel-toed boots. I made a point of showing no expression.

"Did you go to Vietnam?" he asked.

I was used to being judged when people asked this. He just seemed curious.

"No," I replied. "Nixon pulled the Marines out by then."

"I thought about joining the Marines, just to go through boot camp," he said. "To see how I'd do. I didn't care about the rest of it, though." He spit more tobacco. "Follow me," he motioned. "We're drilling. For uranium. This ain't Texas. I'll start you off mixing mud. You ever mixed mud before?"

"No."

"You got college. You'll figure it out."

I hated hearing how I would figure things out. I didn't on our farm. It drove my daddy crazy. I'm not very mechanically inclined.

Mixing mud was easy to do. You dumped a fifty-pound sack of some mixture they called mud into a trough with water, and stirred. Almost like mixing cement except the result was a soupy plastic. We did this into the night. It was ten before they finally let us go home. A lanky guy who came up to my shoulders, with dark hair cropped at his earlobes and an Abraham Lincoln beard, walked up to me.

"You the new guy?" he asked, in a strong Mexican accent. His accent surprised me because he had white skin. Another one not friendly. Nobody on the crew so far had been. "I'm Jose," he said without offering his hand. "I work for Kerr Construction too. Everybody

5

else on the crew already left. We come in two double-cabin pickups, but everyone else left at six." He pointed. "We have that old Chevy pickup to get home. You drive."

"I don't know how to get back."

"I'll get you on the highway," Jose instructed. "Then follow it to town. Wake me up when we get there. I'll tell you how to get the rest of the way."

I've been in college too long. Some idealistic notion told me to be patient, but my instincts said to tell this joker where to go. *Wake him up, indeed.* But in some ways I liked him doing that. Being new, I was anxious and feeling out of place. *Go ahead, piss me off. It settles the nerves.*

Jose needed a ride home when we got back to town. Good. I needed a shower. His wife and new baby boy were in bed when we got there. I wasn't just dirty and grimy, I had this mud stuff on me, too. On my hands and face and on my clothes. Goo. I felt plastic-coated. Jose wasn't pleased, but he let me in. I didn't bother with the shower but washed at his sink.

I found a city park after leaving Jose's and drove to the curb, changed clothes in the back of the truck, unrolled my sleeping bag, meditated, and went to sleep.

My Marine days weren't that far behind. Though I wasn't a combat veteran, every Marine is a rifleman first, no matter what military job they get assigned. That means a lot of drilling, firing, running, marching, and camping out. We camped out at Camp Pendleton in a desert environment like this, and it was so cold at night we had to sleep in full combat gear, including boots, and with two blankets. Coyotes would raid our grounds looking for scraps. So, in spite of getting soft in college lately, what I was doing now was really a step up.

****

I got up with the sun. Once at work, they put me to laying irrigation pipes. That beat the hell out of mixing mud. I used to lay pipes with my daddy on our farm, except the pipes at Kerr Construction were more permanent, and we bolted the joints together instead of just hooking them.

People still weren't friendly. Up to now I was one of two whites, not counting the ones who owned and ran the company. But that had nothing to do with the competition going on among the workers. Not to see who won but who was tough and competent enough to keep from getting fired. Three dollars an hour, bottom-of-the-barrel work, and you had to hustle to keep from losing your job.

"Hey, College," Doug shouted from his pickup. "What's your name again?" I looked up after placing a pipe down. "Come here a minute," he barked.

There was another guy in the pickup too. A huge, reddish-brown-skinned guy with the high cheekbones of a Navajo. He wore a red bandana tied around his head like some Geronimo character. His biceps were as big as my thighs.

"You're going to be here all day," Doug instructed me. "We're bringing you some more pipe and will place them about a quarter mile down the road. You're going to lay these out all the way till you get to that electric post back there on that hill." He pointed behind me. "That's about a mile. I want them in a straight line. You got thirty minutes for your lunch break, then get everybody going again." Before I thought of any questions, he drove away.

"Hey," I shouted, "you just ran over my lunch box."

"What's it doing in the road?" he shouted back. The rest of the crew, behind me, snickered.

"There's no road," I yelled, managing to not shout the four-letter words that came to mind. "I had it out of the way." I knew he didn't hear me.

My salami sandwich now had tire-tread marks on it, and what was left of the bread was black and caked with dirt. My Mounds bar was flat as a penny on a railroad track. I picked up the sandwich, threw away the bread, dusted off the salami the best I could, and ate it.

I seemed to be in charge. *It must be my college degree, but I only just got here. I have no idea what the hell I'm doing. I don't want to be in charge. It doesn't take college to do construction,* I whined inside. *It takes knowing how. I don't know how,* I whined further.

We quit at five, and this time I got to town in time for a cold beer and pizza. And a shower. Not really. I had to settle for a gas station restroom, which meant just another rinse. While there, I took the time to hand wash my dirty clothes in the sink.

****

"McIlhenny," Doug said the next morning, before we loaded up the pickups to go to work. "Come here." The huge guy with him yesterday turned out to be the field foreman and was with him again. "You just got here, and I guess you don't want to stay."

What is this all about? My look echoed my thought.

"After I left you yesterday," he sneered at me, "instead of doing what I told you to do, you just sat

8

around. You don't sit around when you're working for the Kerr Construction Company."

Everybody denies when accused. I didn't want to be like everybody else, but this pissed me off. "I didn't just sit around, Doug."

"Don't give me that."

"Did the pipe get laid or not?"

"When you finish one job you start something else," he spewed out.

"The pipe got laid and I didn't just sit around."

"Well, one of the foremen for Moriah Energy saw you just sitting down on a pipe most of the afternoon."

"No, he didn't," I sneered back.

"Are you calling him a liar? I wouldn't call him a liar if I were you."

"I'm not calling anybody a liar," I said, "but I didn't sit on any pipe half the afternoon. I didn't sit at all, and I'll tell whoever to their face."

"You're one of two whites laying pipe, and you're the tall one."

"So the man said it was me?"

"Plus the other white guy has long, black hair. So, you tell me how a tall white guy with short blond hair was seen just screwing around and it's not you."

"Well, I don't know what to tell you." I sounded arrogant, but didn't care. "I barely even took a break, much less sat around half the afternoon."

"I'm not going to lose this contract," Doug scowled.

"If that's what he said, I want to talk to him."

"He doesn't take lip," Doug said as he spit tobacco on the ground for emphasis. He wasn't convinced, but it made him think.

9

"Dalhart worked the whole afternoon," Jose said, walking up to us. "I was blue topping nearby, and I saw the crew. I don't know what the Moriah man thinks he saw, but Dalhart worked."

"You make sure you do," Doug said, unapologetically, before going to his pickup. The field foreman looked at me just before getting in with Doug and smirked, giving me the feeling I did well, that I met some kind of approval.

"Kick his ass, Dalhart," Jose said, as we walked back to the pickups that would take us to work. "Someone needs to put him in his place."

"He's just doing his job," I answered, surprised at myself for taking up for him.

"Kick his ass," a Navajo laborer said as we reached the others. "You're big. You're a kick-ass Marine."

Is that what you do when you're big here? Kick the boss' ass?

****

I was in a routine. Work, find a place to wash up, eat, read, maybe go to a movie, meditate in the dark in the back of Desperado, and go to bed. But I needed something more now. Phase one was over somehow.

"Hey, Dalhart," the owner of my favorite restaurant said as he came to my table. "How's your day?"

"Hot," I said with a chuckle. "Already feel better now that I'm here. Hope your cook's not on strike."

He smiled, then put on a serious look. "You hear about what happened at the copper mine?" he asked.

I shook my head no.

"Navajo boy. The copper mine caved in where he worked, and he was killed. Just yesterday he sat in the very chair you're sitting in now. He was the nicest guy. I'm still down about it."

"I didn't hear anything about the copper mine," I said in sympathy. "I'm sorry to hear this."

"He went to our church, too. Just the nicest guy."

"I almost worked at that copper mine when I got here a couple of weeks ago," I said. "They took me deep into the shaft to see if I'd panic, before they would hire me. I didn't panic, but I didn't like it."

"It might have been you in that shaft when it collapsed today," he mused. "Listen, I'll leave the menu with you, unless you know what you want."

"Leave it," I said. "Don't know what I want."

"Carmen will be your waitress. It's her first day back. She used to work here a couple of years ago. She's back from North Carolina. Had a messy divorce."

I had just begun reading when I heard, "Would you like a glass of water?" and looked up. She was Mexican, with dark-brown skin, and beautiful. Not just gorgeous, she had an aura. Who the hell would divorce her?

"Are you Carmen?" I asked.

"How did you know?"

"Your boss." Right in front of her I felt myself melt as her smile penetrated my senses.

"That son of a gun," she said with a wink. "Well, you know who I am now. I'll be your waitress. Oh, yes. I already asked you, but you didn't answer. Would you like a glass of water? And I can take your order, too, if you're ready?"

"Yes to both. I'll take your special for today."

"The enchiladas?"

"Yeah."

11

She returned with a pitcher of water and an empty glass for me. I watched the serious look on her face as she seemed to struggle reaching my table. Her hand trembled ever so slightly as she poured. I tried reading the book I'd brought, but couldn't pay attention to it even after she left. I watched her from the corner of my eye as she walked to the kitchen and back, cleaned tables, and handed new customers a menu. I forced myself to refocus on the book. But I couldn't remember anything the book said.

Suddenly I heard a crash and looked up at the next table. She'd knocked over the glass of water while she poured. She gave an apology to the lady and then glanced at me, smiling shyly. "I'm so clumsy today," she said just above a whisper.

I still couldn't concentrate on my book. Then another crash. It was from another table, and now there were two puddles on the floor. I grinned her way as if embarrassed for her. This time she apologized to me before she did the customer.

"I'll be right back," she said as she rushed by my table. "I can't believe this."

I heard myself humming the words to the Marty Robbins song "El Paso." Felina, that was the girl in the song. Now I knew why the doomed cowboy in the song fell so strongly for the Mexican maiden named Felina.

"I'm better," she laughed as she walked by my table to clean up the mess close by. She kept looking up at me as she stooped to sop up the water.

I put my book away. To even pretend reading was a distraction. I didn't stare at her, but I wanted to be able to think about her freely.

"Here's your enchiladas," she said a short time

later. "They're not as good as mine. Don't dare tell I said that."

"Good to be back?" I asked her. "Your boss said you lived in North Carolina."

"It's awkward now," she said wearing a pained expression. "I guess in his biological sketch—" She stopped mid-sentence, realized what she'd said, and blushed slightly. "I mean, biographical sketch. I guess in his biographical sketch of me he said why I'm back."

She didn't have an accent. All the Mexicans back home had accents.

"Yeah," I answered. "Sorry to hear it."

"I have to find my way again, so I'm living with my mom for awhile," she said still wearing the pained expression.

"It happens. I'm not divorced, and I'm living in the back of a panel truck."

"Why's that?"

"I just came from Texas and needed a job. I didn't have any money."

"How long have you been here?"

"A couple of weeks."

"That's enough time to get a place."

"It feels too much like staying. I was like that when I lived in Houston, too, and that was for two years."

"You lived in the back of a panel truck in Houston for two years?"

"Oh no." I grinned. "I had an apartment. But I never bought a bed. I slept on the floor the whole time. Afraid to commit. Then went back to college to get my degree."

"You have a college degree and you live in the back of a panel truck in Gallup, New Mexico?"

13

"Yep. Home's where I hang my hat."

"Do you know your way around Gallup yet?" she chirped.

"I suppose."

"I can show you around."

I almost heard myself swallow.

"I'd like that." I hoped I wasn't blushing. "Nobody has, yet."

"Sure, I'd love to." Her bright smile returned. "How about tonight?"

"Yeah. Yes. Yeah."

"Hey, why don't we just go to a movie?" she asked, her smile even broader now. "There's a movie on about Woody Guthrie, at the cinema. He's like you except he didn't have any college."

I looked at her quizzically. "How am I like him?"

"He hopped freight trains, you live in a van...I don't know." She laughed.

I'd seen the movie the previous night, to tell the truth, but wanted to see it with her. "Yeah, let's go."

"You don't have a date or anything?" she asked shyly.

"Me? No." *I'd get rid of her for you anyway,* I thought to myself wickedly.

I didn't meditate when I got home from the movie, thinking of her. I barely slept the whole night. At the movie and on the drive to her mom's house I behaved myself and wondered why. I wanted to pounce, every second with her, and the only reason I didn't wasn't because I was a gentleman. It was because I felt so shy and so vulnerable. So cowardly. But how was I not going to pounce the next time? And there was going to be a next time. We both knew it. Neither one of us made plans for a next time, but I was going back to that same restaurant, and we were going back to the same movie, or whatever else happened.

All night long until time to get up, even in my sleep, that's all I thought about. Seeing her in the restaurant after work and going somewhere afterwards. And probably pouncing. Except I was also a gentleman, so I wasn't sure I'd really pounce. But I wasn't going to be shy anymore, for sure. Amen.

****

"We got us a new guy," the one that hired me said to Doug the next day as he walked beside a short, skinny guy. "He'll be working with us as a laborer."

Somehow I inherited this guy. I had to teach him things I didn't know, and he was dumber than me about them.

"That pole is bent, McIlhenny," Doug yelled as he drove by where we were building a fence. "I know I said I wanted them in line, but I didn't mean bend them to get them lined up. Didn't you use the level?"

"They're straight, Doug. I used the level."

"They're not straight," he sneered, "they're bent. I'm glad you're big and strong, but don't bend the poles to get them in line with one another. I thought you went to college. I thought you grew up on a farm. Did you bend the poles on your farm?"

"Probably." I laughed. I hated being stupid, but it was funny, too. I had been through such with my daddy.

Doug looked to see if I was being a smart ass. I put on my guilty face for him, which made me look even more like a smart ass. But I knew he wasn't going to fire me. He liked me, I could tell. The huge guy that was field foreman stood next to him and scoped me out. His name was Ira Hays Moonseeker. One of the few Navajos with position. He lit up a cigar and grinned my way, then followed Doug back to the pickup.

I thought work would never end. I was anxious to see Carmen again. I didn't have a watch, which irritated me because I was dying to know the time. I didn't ask anyone with a watch either, afraid I'd end up telling them why I was so impatient to finish work today. I was tempted to ask the time every five minutes, but managed not too. Somehow. The sun was the only clue I had. It seemed like the Old Testament at Jericho the way it just hung up in the sky immobile for hours at a time.

The new worker came in handy for some things. At least for me. He lived with a couple of guys in an old house and said he'd let me use his shower when we came in from work. Now I could consistently freshen up at the end of the day with a nice warm shower instead of washing out of a sink.

****

I looked serious and aloof as I walked into the restaurant after work. Carmen saw me and stopped dead in her tracks just to stare as I walked to an open table. She then returned to her work after a wink my direction.

"Enchiladas," I said when she came to my table to place my order.

"They aren't the special today," she said.

"Then I'll have them at your place. You invited me last night, remember?"

She puckered her lips to keep from smiling. "Rather bold today, aren't we?"

16

"To make up for lost time," I answered. "I blew last night trying to be polite. I want to get to know you."

"I enjoyed last night," she said with a nod. "Especially all your comments about Woody Guthrie and all after the movie. You know so much about him."

"Yeah, I like those times and his music. But I was nervous, too. And shy."

"Shy? You don't seem the type. What's there to be shy about?"

"You." I sighed. "I was shy, and talking gibberish helped. I want to get to know you now. I loved being with you. So, I'll take your invitation. Okay?"

"My mother wants to meet you," she said. "We had a long talk about you this morning. Someone got my mind off the divorce I just went through. She wants to meet him. And see if he's all she's hearing."

"What's she been hearing?" I asked quizzically.

"What I told her."

I kept waiting for what that was.

"You just wait on me here until I'm off work," she said. "You'll get the gist when we get home. Have a beer or two on me while you wait. Read your book. Keep yourself occupied for a couple more hours."

Her mother's house was a two-bedroom wood-frame yellow cottage with a screened-off front porch. A middle-aged dark-skinned woman, slightly overweight, let us in. She was the same height as Carmen, I guessed five feet four, which was tall for a Mexican-American woman. She still had good looks, with occasional streaks of gray in her hair.

"Mother's been a widow since I was in high school," Carmen explained. "My dad was killed in a car accident. I have a younger sister, but she's in Germany. She married a soldier from Albuquerque."

"Have a seat on the couch," Carmen's mother said. "I prepared you some enchiladas after my daughter called me on the phone tonight. I'll bring them in after I microwave them. They got cold. Eat all you want."

"You know," I commented to Carmen, "the Mexican-Americans back home all have accents and they seem just as Mexican as they are American. You just seem an American with brown skin to me. It's almost confusing."

"Is that okay with you?" she asked. "Would you rather me talk differently?"

"No, I love it. Even the Mexican-Americans in college had accents. Not strong, but something. You don't have any accent at all."

"I don't know, I'm just me. Some of us here talk with an accent. Those just here or a generation removed. Most of my friends are just as American as can be. I have a lot of Anglo friends. I don't even know Spanish."

Carmen got up to leave but looked back toward me at the entrance to a bedroom. "I'm going to take a quick shower," she said. "I won't be long. I get all sweaty, and there's a tobacco stench on my clothes, too. So many smoke, you know."

She hadn't returned when, several minutes later, her mother came out with two plates of enchiladas. One, I assumed, was for Carmen.

"Go ahead and start without her," Carmen's mother said. "I know you must be starving. My daughter tells me you're from Texas and that you work as a laborer even though you have a college degree."

"Yes, ma'am."

"That's strange. So many here don't have any college, much less a degree. If I had education, I would be so far away."

"I like it here," I replied.

"It's okay," she admitted. "It's home. The people are nice, and there are some exotic landscapes around. But I would think you could say the same thing about Texas. I don't understand what brings you here."

"I wanted something I've never seen before."

"Go to Alaska. Or Hawaii. I would love to go to Hawaii."

"So would I," I said, smiling. "I might do that someday."

"You and Carmen just met yesterday?"

"Yes, ma'am. Last night was the first time we went out together."

"She really likes you. You seem nice, and you're tall and muscular, have an education. What do you see in my daughter? Am I being too forward?"

"I don't know yet the attraction about her," I answered. "It's just there. She's got a spark, she's pretty, she seems really bright."

"Carmen seems bright to you? She was a terrible student. That's why she's a waitress. I told her to study and go to college and make something of herself. But here she is a waitress and just got through a divorce. I don't know if that's very smart."

"She seems very smart to me. It's in her. Some people just don't like books. Or some don't like the structure and discipline of a classroom. She's smart. I see it."

Her mother smiled.

"Who's smart?" Carmen asked, as she reentered the room. I nibbled intensely at my lower lip as a smile eased through. She had her hair wrapped in a bright white towel and was wearing a white bathrobe made of the same coarse material. I loved the contrast of her dark brown skin against the whiteness of her robe and the thick blackness of the strands of hair escaping at the edge of the towel wrapping her head like a crown. What had taken me so long to grasp the cosmetic allure of dark skin, I wondered. She was the sexiest woman I'd ever seen. As much as I now felt liberated, I cursed the trap of a past that had kept me from knowing all of this sooner.

"My goodness, Daughter," Carmen's mother said. "Girlie, you can't come into a room with a man you just met, dressed like that. I have rules in this house."

"I know, Mother, but I didn't feel like getting dressed again. I have a slip on under this. Can't I relax a bit, please?"

"It's against my better judgment," her mother said before turning back to me. "You understand why I have rules, don't you? What's your name? Dalhart, isn't it?"

"Yes, ma'am. I absolutely understand."

"We can't have mischief," she explained further. "This is my home. It has sanctity."

"I understand that," I said.

"Your food's getting cold, Dalhart," her mom said, relaxing again. "Come, Daughter, he waited for you. He's a true gentleman. Both of you eat now, or I'll have to warm it up again. It spoils the texture after a while."

Carmen's mother left us to ourselves as we sat on the couch next to each other, far enough away to be polite but close enough for me to feel her energy. And body heat. Occasionally, our elbows bumped as we cut the food with our forks while eating awkwardly from the plates on our laps. They had a dining table in the kitchen. I didn't know why we were eating on the couch, but was glad. It was cozy this way, and informal. When I thought perhaps this coziness was the reason why we were here instead of the dining room, it made me feel all the more relaxed.

Shortly after we finished eating, her mom reentered the living room. "I'm going to bed, Carms. I have to get up early to get to work. It was nice to have met you, Dalhart, and I'm happy we have our understanding. Our mutual trust, I'm saying."

"Mother," Carmen sighed. "Dalhart doesn't have a place to shower and then sleeps in his van. Can he shower here and then sleep on our couch? Please? He is a guest here in Gallup. Please let's help him."

"Oh, Carmen, no," I said. "I'm fine. I couldn't even consider imposing. I've already showered anyway."

She whispered pointedly, as if telling me to mind my own business, "I'm talking about from now on."

"People will gossip, Carms," her mother replied. "I know that sounds like a lame reason to you, but it matters. This is a small town, and you just arrived back and with a fresh divorce."

"They can't live our lives for us, Mother. He needs a place. If you are worried about us, I promise to behave. I'm a grown woman, but I will behave for you in your house that you are letting me stay in. But please be fair."

"Carmen, I'm fine," I said, feeling awkward. "I've been doing this for two weeks now. I have a place to shower now, and I sleep well in my panel truck."

"You understand, don't you, Dalhart?" Carmen's mother looked sheepishly at me. "My daughter just back from a divorce and here comes another Anglo staying in our house before the ink is dry on the papers."

"I fully understand," I said to her. I looked at Carmen. "Carmen, it's important to me. I want to get to know you before I impose on you."

Carmen gave a quick, deliberate, grudging nod with her head and stared straight ahead, holding her thoughts.

"Good night, ma'am," I said to her mother. "I won't stay much longer. We're just getting to know one another and want to talk a bit more."

"I understand, Dalhart," her mother answered. "I'm very glad to get to know you, and you've brought some excitement back into my daughter's life. Good night, the two of you. I'm glad I can trust you and depend on you."

"Good night, Mother," Carmen said. "I do understand. Just disappointed."

She then turned to me, and it seemed as if her black eyes glowed. "You are so sweet to her," Carmen said, smiling. "You show respect. It's so old-fashioned, but it's nice. I like it. I can't believe I'm saying that."

"You can't believe you're saying you like old-fashioned?"

"I suppose," she explained. "That must sound rather loose to you. Maybe I'm a bit loose. I had fun growing up. I'm not saying I was promiscuous, but I had some fun. But here I am now. My marriage was based on fun, and it wasn't so much fun after all. Old-fashioned seems rather refreshing for a change."

"I'm not going away," I said. "I kind of like going slowly."

"Yeah, well." She sighed. "All that said, I couldn't believe we didn't even kiss last night. I kept waiting for this Texas guy to seduce me. You were the perfect gentleman. Like some knight in shining armor. I hated you for it." She laughed.

"I'm not as honorable as you might think. My hormones were raging. Still are. I felt nervous and vulnerable more than honorable. But if I had felt a hot juicy kiss on my lips last night, I might have not gone home. So I talked about Woody Guthrie instead."

"I'm getting hot just hearing that, Dalhart. One of the worst things about a divorce is that suddenly there's no man in your life anymore. No affection, no rapport." Her smile broadened. "Or even fun. Or raging hormones. Are we going to kiss tonight? Can you handle it?" She turned away giggling girlishly. "Can I?"

"I want to go slowly," I repeated. "Even without your mother's words, but especially now because of her. But, yeah, I'd love a kiss."

Her expression turned serious, but soft. She tilted her head slightly and leaned toward me, teasing my lips with hers at first and then planting them fully, while at the same time stroking my cheek with her fingertips. I placed my hand behind her neck and pulled her more firmly into me. I somehow had forgotten the electric-like charge of such an embrace. How did I live without it so long?

We released the kiss and leaned back into the couch holding hands.

"I got the hots for you, Dalhart," she said rubbing

her thumb softly on the back of my hand. "Tell me the same thing. I want to hear you say it to me."

"Yeah," I said, nodding my head.

"Yeah, what? I want to hear you tell me you got the hots for me. Tell me in those words. Those same exact words."

I looked at her awkwardly. "I feel all that," I said. "Just let me feel it."

"What are we going to do?" she asked. "All this honor between us we're suddenly stuck with."

"It'll work out, Carmen. There's a lot you don't know about me. I need to go slowly. It'll work out."

I managed to meditate when I got back to the van, but it was clouded, and intruded upon by thoughts of her. Her. That's what I thought about all night long. That and us.

****

"How do you know Spanish?" Jose asked as we dug a trench next to a water pump.

"I don't know very much," I replied.

"You understand sometimes when I talk to the others," he commented.

"I learned a little from growing up on the border. We had a lot of first-generation from Mexico on our farm, and a lot of illegals. I should know more. My daddy knows Spanish fluently."

"Why does a college man come here?" he asked.

"I used to work in computers in Houston, when I got out of the Marines. Before I went back to college to finish my degree. It was the worst time of my life."

"Worse than this?" he asked me, cracking a smile. A smile from a coworker. That was a breakthrough.

"This does suck," I said, "but when it came time to

choose a career, I couldn't make up my mind what to do. The thought even scared me. I'm looking for my place."

"It's not here." He laughed.

"I like it here okay. For now."

"I'm here because there's no other place for me," Jose explained. "Otherwise I wouldn't be here. No matter what you say, college boy, I think you're crazy."

"You've got it made here, Jose. Doug likes you. He's teaching you to use heavy equipment. You'll make bucks."

"That's why I'm here, nothing else. I'm illegal too, just like your hands on your *patron* daddy's farm. There's nothing for me back home. As bad as this is, it's something. And then I see you, and you have everything, and you're here too. *Mi no sabe, hombre.*"

"Except for your accent, you speak perfect English," I noted. "How long you been here?"

"Three years," he answered. "President Carter is talking about amnesty for illegal aliens that have been here for so long. I thought about applying, but then I'm afraid the Border Patrol will pick me up."

"I figured you were illegal," I said.

"Almost everybody except the Navajos," he explained. "And now here comes a white college guy from Texas. *Mi no sabe* at all."

"How did you learn English like that in three years? Man, you make me ashamed. I'm horrible at Spanish."

"Survival," Jose replied.

"The other illegals don't know English," I said. "Maybe a couple do."

"They don't care. They make a few bucks and go

back home. There's no going back for me. I have my wife, illegal wife, and my baby boy, legal baby boy."

"Where's back for you?" I asked.

"Durango. I worked for a *patron* like my papa does even now. That is no life. I tried boxing. I won a few, but unless you're a champion you get your brains beat out for nothing. I fought bulls for a couple of years."

"You were a bullfighter, Jose?"

"I was even good. I had sponsors. But then I got my wife pregnant. We weren't married then. So, I had to get married and raise a kid. It's better to come to America. And meet a *gringo* crazier than me. I'm talking about you, *hombre*."

"You mean minimum wage in America is better than bullfighting at entry level?"

"For sure." Jose sighed. "I'm alive. I might be dead if I stayed in the bullring. And now I learn to use heavy equipment. I can make it if I become legal."

"I used to work the fields with illegals," I related. "We called them wetbacks, for swimming the Rio Grande to get to Texas. You can't say that now. Anyway, we barely paid our illegals anything, but we gave them a shack for free. They not only saved but sent money back to their families. One guy was like my big brother. Then, with another hand, we were both disking a field. At quitting time he looked at me from his tractor, smiled, then went home and asked my daddy to borrow our twenty-two rifle to go rabbit hunting. We found his body the next morning. He blew his brains out with that twenty-two."

"Hey, *amigo*. Dalhart." Two of the others called out to me as they walked to the pickup for a break. "*Merienda*," they said. "Dalhart, we have for you."

26

They wrapped a tortilla around three chili peppers and handed it to me. I bit into it and felt something bite back. *Hellfire reincarnated.* I wanted to scream, except I was from Texas.

I looked at them in disbelief as they munched away on theirs. I could not let Mexicans beat me, but my nose kept running. I pictured steam coming out of my ears like in some cartoon as my eyes watered. I tore off a piece of tortilla without any chili pepper and tossed it into my mouth to pacify what was left of my tongue.

Jose took it all in. "You're a crazy one." He shook his head and grinned. "You try hard, for a *gringo*."

****

It felt commonplace now, even though it had been just a week since I first started seeing Carmen. I would go to the house of my work colleague to shower, then to the restaurant where she worked. If she wasn't in the dining area when I arrived, I would seat myself and wait until she appeared. Otherwise, I'd walk up to her, even if she was in the process of taking an order. We would always kiss. Nothing dramatic, considering where we were, but a definite show of affection. A continuum for our territorial claims on each other, as well as a renewal of commitment. That's what it was now, commitment. We just had no idea what we were going to do about it.

They had a jukebox where she worked. Somewhere during the process of me waiting for her to finish work, each of us would play a song on it. Something to show what kind of mood we were in. Perhaps a message directed at the other one that was to be figured out. A moody sentimental song, or an energizing Beatles song, or a he-done-her-wrong type of song. And before we went home, either during the song we played or one we got off to that someone else played, we'd dance, right there in the diner in front of everyone. It got to where people in the restaurant encouraged it, even by playing a song of their choice, hoping we would dance to it.

Carmen didn't live far from where she worked. We could have walked. But that was part of the courtship now, me driving her to her mom's, then staying awhile. I still left the house when our evening together was over. That part hadn't changed. It wasn't so special now to me, being so pure. It seemed more like a duty. That was a bad sign. Something was going to give somewhere, I was sure.

****

I hated working Saturdays, especially since it took away from time with Carmen, but I needed the money. Usually the work on a Saturday was especially boring, though. So I was glad when Doug pulled me away from the others as we policed the area. He led me to the workshop.

"I need you to hold this bar up," he said. "You better have rubber soles on your boots, because this may shock a bit when I weld."

I felt the red hot filings hit my arm as I looked at our shadows from the electrical flares spewing out of the welding rod. Then suddenly I felt an electrical jolt on my shoulder. I turned to look just as Doug poked me again with the tip of the rod, knowing I wouldn't drop the bar I was holding. Then he did it yet again.

"Ow!" I yelped, dropping the steel bar onto the floor to defy him.

"Is it hot?" He laughed as he put down the welding rod. "Let's go to my place and landscape. Get the

28

others. We'll put something on the grill and have a beer."

We laid out plots of carpet grass and dug a flowerbed in his back yard while Doug got the grill going. He still wore his hard hat but was shirtless. He had a new four-bedroom brick house, and I could feel the pangs of envy as I dug in the yard. I'd lived like that most of my life. But the pangs were there anyway. Why did some people have and others not? And why was I asking a question like this all of a sudden?

"Everybody have a beer," Doug invited as we put down our shovels and entered his patio area. "That's enough work for today."

Ira dug out a wad of tobacco from his cheek and threw it into a bush before getting a can of beer from the cooler.

"In Texas you leave the chaw in, don't you?" Doug ribbed. "When you drink a beer, I mean."

"McIlhenny doesn't chew tobacco." Ira snorted. "It's beneath him. Are you sure you're from Texas? You sure you're a Marine? Hell, Doug, the other day we came back to town and I saw him pick up a *Playboy* off the seat of the truck. I thought, hey, this guy's human after all. But I'll be damned if he didn't read instead of look at the pictures."

"It was on Rhodesia," I answered. "They're on the verge of having a black President."

"Rhodesia?" Ira howled. "Who gives a damn? Ain't you got hormones?"

"But he knows everything," Jose said. "Ask him anything. Anything about this whole universe."

"He doesn't know how to build a fence." Doug laughed.

"Who was the nineteenth President?" Ira asked.

"Rutherford B. Hayes," I answered. "I wrote a paper about him in high school. The Democrat Samuel Tilden should have won the election, but the radical Republicans managed to rig the Louisiana vote. That got it thrown into the Republican-controlled House of Representatives."

"Shut up," Ira said. "Shut the hell up. Who cares?"

"Don't ask." I smirked.

"I won't," Ira returned. "You wrote a paper in high school on it. Give me a break. Hell, I couldn't write in high school."

"You still can't." Doug snickered.

"Kiss my ass, boss," Ira came back.

"McIlhenny," Doug said, "after we eat, you and me are going at it. I want to see if I can beat a Marine. The only reason I hired you was because you were bigger and uglier than me and you're a Marine."

"I ain't ugly, Doug. And I don't want to fight."

"You got to earn your pay," he challenged.

I saw a bottle of whiskey freshly opened on the panel of the grill. "Is that yours?" I asked.

"Yeah," he replied.

I walked over and guzzled down half of the bottle in one gulp.

"What the hell are you doing?" he shrieked.

"Getting ready to kick your ass and get it over with," I answered.

"The hell, you say," he sneered. "Come on, then."

I loved this guy. He was so predictable. Perfect timing, perfect wording. I walked up to him and saw him double his fists. I grabbed a wad of his chest hair and jerked it. A large white patch appeared in the middle of his carpet of black hair. He howled in pain and lunged for me. I moved to the side, stuck out my foot, and pushed him down, then swigged more of his whiskey.

"On the other hand, I enjoy a good brawl now and then." I smirked. "Good food, good fight, good whiskey. You throw a swell party, Doug."

"Don't do that again," he said, getting up, trying to appreciate what I had done. "We'll settle this someday."

****

The next weekend I had off. Since we didn't always have Saturdays off, I wanted to take advantage now that I had one free. Plus, I just got paid. I wanted to do something. And with Carmen. Just get away. Just the two of us.

"The Grand Canyon's not far," Carmen said as we got out a map. "I don't know how fast we can get there in your Desperado," she added with a laugh, "but we should make it in about four hours, if we don't stop much. It's a great drive, and even if we don't hike down, the view from the canyon rim takes your breath away."

The thought appealed to me, but I studied the map to see what other options we had. I had never been to this part of the country and everything excited me.

"My grandma lived in Pueblo," I commented as we looked things over.

"Pueblo Indians or Pueblo, Colorado?" she asked. "You have to be more specific in this part of the country, you know."

"Colorado," I said, approving of her request for detail. "I spent parts of some summers there. Grandma lived on a farm with no electricity or plumbing. My grandpa, actually step-grandpa, plowed by mule. I felt like Daniel Boone when I was with them. We could see Pikes Peak from their log cabin."

"Is she still alive?" Carmen asked me. "We'd be pushing it to get there and back in one weekend. It would be basically drive up, say hello, spend the night, and drive back."

"She lives in Denver now that Grandpa died," I explained. "That's okay. I've been there. Let's go somewhere new."

My thoughts perked as I zeroed my finger onto a spot on the map, then gleefully looked at her.

"Monument Valley's not much farther away than the Grand Canyon," I said. "Just a different direction."

"Everybody wants to see the Grand Canyon, and the object of my affection here, meaning you, goes the other way," she said, shaking her head. "Why Monument Valley?"

"Haven't you seen those John Wayne movies? They're eerily spiritual."

"Spiritual?" She scoffed. "Monument Valley is spiritual to you? It's desert. We have that around here."

I nodded. "It's like ghosts live there. It has soul."

"Ghosts are spiritual to you?"

"It's this wide open setting," I tried explaining further, "with sculptures carved by God. Sacred. And not only that, John Wayne had this special style. While the rest of Hollywood was making B movies, he had depth and setting. Command. At least his better movies did. Like at Monument Valley. And on top of that he's the one who took up for the serviceman during the Vietnam War."

"A lot of people took up for servicemen during the Vietnam War," Carmen corrected.

"But he stood up for us. He went out of his way to do this. He challenged those that were down on us, those burning the flag, and making Marines out as baby killers."

She studied me for a moment. "You seem scarred or something. I heard of guys coming back from Vietnam being scarred, but you seem scarred and you didn't go."

"I wanted to go." I struggled for the words. "I believed in the war. So, no, I wasn't scarred from the war. I was scarred, if that's the word, from the mindset. From our generation. And even though I think people have a right to dissent, they were burning the flag, and taking up for Communism, and making us out to be the aggressor. We talked European powers into giving up their colonies, but were accused of holding on to them, just because we were trying to keep the Communists out. Did you see what the North Vietnamese did when they took over South Vietnam? And everywhere else?"

"I don't want to talk politics," she said meekly.

"Me either," I answered, apology in my voice. "I just appreciated John Wayne for his stand, and somehow there's all this about Monument Valley, too. It represents something to my psyche somehow. I want to find out more why it does. It has character. Let's go. We'll go to the Grand Canyon next time."

Carmen rubbed my upper arm affectionately. "You said the magic words, Dalhart. You said 'next time.' There'll be a next time, and we'll go there then."

"Monument Valley and the Grand Canyon look the same distance on the map," I said refocusing my attention on how to get there.

"It's not direct, though," she explained. "But I think we can get there in the same amount of time."

"What are these little fiber-like lines on the map?" I moaned. "Just before we get to the famous mesas in the John Wayne movies."

She stared at them, trying to figure it out with me. "Maybe farm-to-market roads," she said. "This is New Mexico and Arizona. Our roads suck eggs. We'll go due north to Shiprock first, that's a good highway, and it's all in New Mexico. But once we turn west into Arizona, it's all desolate terrain. That's when those fibers for roads on the map begin. They might even be dirt roads. It happens in this part of New Mexico, too. It leads us to a sparse area and then we're on our own. Nobody lives there, I guess."

"We'll stock up with food and drink," I instructed, "and extra water for the radiator, just in case."

On the way, we passed by Window Rock. I recognized it because the Indian reservation where Kerr contracted was near there. All these eroded hills and giant rocks. Like the roadrunner and coyote cartoons I used to watch. New Mexico was the world's best-kept secret, I decided.

The town of Shiprock had an eroded hill that did indeed look like a ship. A sandstone hill, I assumed, that had worn down to a God-made sculpture of a ship floating on just enough rock to keep it afloat. *How long has it been here*, I wondered as I stared, *and how much longer before it crashes? Will they change the name of the town when it does?*

The edge of Monument Valley was less than an hour due west of Shiprock. And now the fun began.

Small paved roads narrowed into a one-lane graded dirt road. Miles of this allowed me near the table-like structures resting on red sand that were prominent in the John Wayne movies. Some of the structures looked like stalagmites.

We were probably breaking some law if we walked up to these mesas. Somehow they were protected, or should be. Between that and being tired, we settled for a small rise of a sand-like dune near the dirt road we were on. I parked my van off to the side of it, sure we were the only human beings around in this heat, and positioned the van in such a way that we could sit at the back with the rear doors open and get a perfect view of the most scenic mesas. We imbibed over a quart of water, then a still-icy soda each, and just stared. That was enough. To just stare.

"I'm part Cherokee," I said to Carmen. "Not enough to lay claim to the heritage, but enough to feel proud. And I feel so proud even though this is Navajo country."

I glanced at her shyly, afraid I looked the fool. She nodded her head supportively, and returned to viewing the mesas in front of us.

"I wish I knew a Cherokee song," I continued, "or any Indian song, for that matter. I want to share this with whatever spirits might be hovering around, as more than a descendent of a white conqueror. But it's okay to be white, too. Now I can make amends somehow, right here, right now, to my Indian side. And live in harmony. I guess. Even though that sounds so hippie."

She shook her head and looked at me mockingly. "You're on a crusade, Dalhart. Still the Marine. You live in a van when you could be starting a career any of the rest of us would die for. It's like you're looking for yourself. But you're so against our generation. You even still use the word 'hippie.' You're so like them, though, you know? Not exactly. But this anti-materialism thing about you is. Yet you hate their lifestyle and politics. I guess the word is complex. You're so damn complex, *mi amour*."

"I hope to have money someday, Carmen. I'm not a back-to-nature freak. People wonder what I'm doing here. Maybe it's my upbringing. On the farm where I worked with my parents, we felt so productive. Me and all the families around and all the kids on those farms working them with their parents. The work was hard, and we'd complain or want better. But now America just wants out. Wealth is new to us. Yet another God-given freedom that we're just not up to. We OD'ed culturally from it."

I looked at her sheepishly as if to apologize. "Sorry," I said. "I get caught up in my thoughts. But can we talk?"

"That's why we're here, Dalhart. It's just the two of us. And the ghosts." She laughed. "It's time to get to know each other more deeply. Like some romantic job interview, you know."

"Yeah," I said, smiling, relating to the way she put things. "Yeah."

She leaned over and kissed me on the cheek, then held my hand. "Go on," she said. "You seem the philosopher. Got me a college guy here. Talk away. I like this. I feel deep all of a sudden."

"So," I continued, trying to reconnect to my thoughts. "We work more for security and materialism than anything else. And we need entertainment so much. To the point of childlike. I'm not knocking the entertainment factor completely. I need entertainment and material things too. But what happens when someone goes to a party or gets drunk? They call it living. And to them it is. Suddenly they have a life, they think. Renewed energy. It's like they've been resurrected from the dead. I never understood why. I was my proudest when I was on our farm, productive. When I had money I spent some of it. Even on entertainment. But it wasn't my life."

"This is a bigger thing for you somehow than the way you were treated in the Marines by this generic group you're calling hippies," she commented.

"Actually, you're right," I said, as I nodded agreement. "But it all seems so intertwined. To me it's this party mentality so prevalent now with us that I'm reacting against. No depth to it. At least not anymore. Maybe there was for awhile, but not for long. It's not just against Marines and the war and corporations going on. The times are against anyone that plays the game. Asian immigrants come over here now that read books. Rich white kids think them nerds the way they study and know math. They laugh or feel threatened by those that come over here to work for the life it provides. And the life most immigrants want is based on family and values, not drugs, sex, and rock-and-roll like seems to be happening to us now. And it's the illegals from Mexico in the fields now that just want a life at all. My daddy worked in other people's fields before he had his own farm. So did the Okies in California that everyone mocks for it."

I turned to look at her for emphasis. As if to

highlight what I was going to say next. "Do you know why the Japanese bombed us at Pearl Harbor on December 7, 1941?"

"We were a threat to them in the Pacific," she answered.

"Yes, but why December 7? It was a Sunday morning. It wasn't because it was a Sunday and we'd all be in church, or relaxing on the beach away from our duties on our day off. It was because Sunday morning comes after Saturday night, and the good old G.I. could be counted on spending what little money he had on getting drunk. Getting drunk to the point of stupor. Totally unprepared to recuperate and fight the surprise attack taking place. Escapism is so engrained in most of our society. Including through religion. Rather than just relate to life and solve problems. Before our generation came along, people used discipline in their lives to overcome escapism. They sensed something better, or were taught there was something better, so they tried to discipline themselves and others to get to that something better. But they never really made the connection. Just had the concept of it. Our generation got rid of the discipline and the ideology."

"Sorry, Dalhart," she said with a grimace. "But you sound like a hippie." She saw my demeanor change as soon as she said it. "Just joking," she chirped, to pacify me. "You're just so disgusted with things."

"I identified with some of the rebellion of my generation in the beginning. But that rebellion also, to most of those doing it, just turned into a party. To me, some of that early rebellion was a breath of fresh air. There was a conformity around in the fifties and early sixties to the point of becoming a robot. I'd just as soon leave the straight jackets for those that are crazy, but we were programmed a lot when we were growing up, to the point where it often felt like a straight jacket for all of us. So I got off to some of the questioning going on in the sixties and the creativity that exploded from it. But then my generation conformed again. Questioned things just enough to adapt to the new thought and conformed to it. Now it's just demands, no questions going on. I guess I'm exaggerating, but I'm not sure."

Carmen stared off toward the mesas as if absorbing the conversation. It was hot, with little breeze, so I retrieved more water from the ice chest.

"I brought my tape cassette player," I said as I returned the water bottle to the melting ice in the chest. "Do you like country music?"

"Some of it," she replied. "Not the hillbilly stuff too much, though."

"I have folk music mixed with it on the tape I brought." I pulled out the cassette player from my backpack that I kept my things in. "The modern ones, not Woody Guthrie."

"You do?" she asked. "Rita Coolidge is my favorite singer. Do you have her?"

I shook my head no.

"Monument Valley is so sparse," I commented as I sat back down beside her. "So…what's the word? Not barren, though it is barren. It's lonely. But proud. It knows something. It's like Stonehenge, except God made it, not us. That's what probably draws me to it the most. Like the monks retreating to the desert for a life of devotion and contemplation."

"I never met anyone like you," she said.

"Is that good or bad?" I asked.

"What the hell do you think? Why else am I here sweating to death looking at sandstone? I want to get to know you. See what rattles my chains for you."

I nodded that I liked her answer. I studied her for a moment and couldn't resist. I kissed her tenderly on the lips, then let it linger to feel her warmth. She kissed me back more deeply and we held it as if in celebration of the moment. We then leaned apart enough to look one another in the eyes, releasing, in the process, one of our arms in order to each touch the other's face with our fingertips.

"I like the sad songs on this tape," I said, just above a whisper. "I like the thought of them even more now that I'm with you. And feel the loneliness I feel so often, but mixed with fulfillment now from being with you. I especially like the tearjerkers. The lonely heartaches. This place gets me in the mood. It allures loneliness here. I love how it seeps to the bone marrow. It's a chance to get to know ourselves here. To hear ourselves think. I even love the pain of loneliness. As long as you're here to reassure me. To cling to pain is self-destructive, but it's cleansing to ride the flow it's on. And now you're riding it with me. I feel so secure."

She looked at me to tease. "That's some heavy stuff there, cowboy."

"It's the cowboy in me, actually," I explained, "that loves all this. That's why I prefer loneliness to being a part of a crowd. But I need to share it with you. Hank Williams is the king of country music loneliness, but I pity the girl who broke the heart of Roy Orbison in his song 'Crying.' He knew beauty she could never imagine. But you know that beauty. It's there in you. You share it with me right back. And Dick Van Arsdale wrote about a lonesome tumbleweed. I love the way Joan Baez sings it. And Kenny Rogers when he sings 'A Stranger In My Place.' Loneliness and heartache are peaceful. And sharing it with you, it's even fulfilling."

"You're like a poet," she said. "With all this coming out in you, I'm so glad we came here."

We lingered in our mood brought on by the desert scene accompanied by the music as if the songs were a musical score to our feelings as we remained in our embrace. When the tape finished, we lingered yet longer in the depth of the silence until the last of the shared loneliness poured out of us.

"Let me change the tape," I said. "Do you like classical music?"

I broke our embrace to change the tape before she could answer.

"On this tape," I explained as if I was a master of ceremonies, "is Beethoven's 'Für Elise' and 'Moonlight Sonata.' And I have Pachelbel's 'Canon in D' and Vivaldi's 'Four Seasons' and Schubert's 'Unfinished Symphony.' I leaned back against the wall of the van as she leaned back against me, sharing my embrace. I stroked her cheek softly with my fingertips as we let ourselves be swayed by the music and the feelings that flowed while we caressed.

"It's religious," she said. "I never liked classical music until now, but it seems religious, really, in this majestic setting we're in."

She looked back toward me as best she could. I kissed her on her neck.

"Are you religious?" she asked. "You talk about how religious you were. Are you still?"

"Yeah," I said, "but in a different way."

41

"What do you mean?"

"I was brought up believing the Bible literally," I explained.

"And now you don't?" she asked.

"When I was in the eighth grade, a friend of mine was killed on his motor scooter on his way to school. We heard the announcement on the speaker in the auditorium just before class. We immediately started praying for him. I'm from the Bible Belt, and we wondered among ourselves if he was in heaven or hell. We were scared just at the thought that what if somehow it was the worst case. The thought gnawed on me. By the time I was a freshman in high school, I didn't believe in hell anymore. Not like in the Bible anyway. Eternal fire for sinners. My friend's death made it personal. If he owed accountability in some way, that was between him and God. But I couldn't see God doing that to anyone, much less to my friend."

"Not even to Hitler?" she asked.

"Not even to Hitler," I replied. "Surely, Hitler had hell to pay, but not like that. Then I started questioning other things."

"I don't know what I believe," she said, clutching my hand possessively. "But I believe. God is too beautiful not to believe in."

I nodded to assure her.

"My favorite story in the Bible," she continued, "is where that girl, I think it was Mary Magdalene, went to the Pharisee's house."

"Simon the Pharisee," I added.

"She wasn't invited," Carmen went on, "and it was like Jesus was there as a status symbol for this Pharisee. What I love about the story is that she wasn't invited, and she felt so unworthy, but she just had to see Jesus. I feel that way a lot. Especially after the divorce. Like I need to crash some Pharisee's party to see Jesus and beg for forgiveness."

"What happened with your marriage?" I asked.

"We were so immature," she explained. "Partying, good times, fun. Go out. That's no reason to marry. He was a life-of-the-party kind of guy, and good looking. He made me feel special. He was just out of the Army. On drugs. I wasn't on drugs, though. Anyway, he knew how to please a girl. Including sexually. Except that sex to him seemed like just another drug. I wanted out of Gallup and he seemed cool. I met him through my sister. He'd been in the Army with her husband. We double-dated once and hit it off. My sister's husband was from Albuquerque."

"And all that fun wasn't enough?" I asked, to fill in the blanks.

"I thought it was. I loved it. For awhile. Had the time of my life. Until he'd get stoned and want every other chick around. I'm not possessive. I thought I wasn't, anyway. But I felt like an old shoe. I came home. We're poor, but even my life in Gallup is better than that. My mom loves me. My mom raised me better. I didn't want her kind of life in Gallup, but I wanted something she gave me. It's so easy to take love for granted. I took my mother and how she loved me for granted my whole life. She's such a simple woman, and we've always been poor. So I decided I wanted more than her kind of life. But this brought it home. She didn't do everything right, but when someone loves you, it seems right anyway. I was desperate for love and appreciation when I came back home. I went to church with her, and the priest talked about Simon the Pharisee, with Mary Magdalene crashing his party to see Jesus. It was like in a movie or a sermon. You know, the way the message seems just for you. So I don't go to church much, but I want that, what the Bible talks about. I want to crash somebody's party and wash the feet of Jesus with my tears and wipe them away with my hair. I want something he has."

She looked back towards me momentarily with a shy smile before turning back around. "You deserve the corn coming out of me now," she said with a grin. "You brought me here, and this is what it's doing to me. So, there you go. The corn's your fault."

"That's what I want out of life too," I said to reassure her and share her mood. "When I first started questioning the Bible, I decided I didn't believe all that about the Garden of Eden, or Jonah and the whale. But then, yeah, like you said, there's just too much beauty. Too much meaning. I don't care anymore if it's literally true or not. It touches me. My favorite story in the Bible is when Jacob wrestled the angel. Maybe it was God he wrestled. It turns out the ancient Hebrews used a lot of puns. Adam means man, for instance, which is derived from Adamah, which means earth, like dirt, not the planet. Israel means one who wrestles with God."

"Are you serious?" She looked up at me, once again showing disbelief. "It means that, it's not just a name? What does Eve mean? Do you know?"

"Eve is more of a modern translation. In the origin of the name she was called Khava, which means life. I guess as in the giver of life."

I felt her body turn rigid. "This blows my mind," she huffed. "How do you know all this stuff?"

"I like knowing the origins of things," I said. "It gives me more perspective. Not just learning a story or memorizing a text. Some depth. Some meaning to it. So, the ancient Hebrew did it for a reason. All the more reason to not take it as history as much as truth."

"Now what the hell does that mean, Dalhart?"

"History isn't the issue," I answered. "The soul is the issue. It can be historically accurate or not. Who cares either way? The meaning is the issue. The meaning is the truth that's laid out for us. But here's Jacob, and he cheats his brother out of his birthright, he flees, he marries the wrong girl, he waits to get the girl he wants, then he wrestles with an angel and won't let go even after his hip is dislocated. I adore that. The passion and the struggle. The determination. The spiritual truth behind it all. That's the important stuff. That's the meat to it."

Carmen nodded her head approvingly. "I love that we met," she said. "I want to believe it really is cosmic. Fate or something. Why aren't you a priest?"

"I'd rather be a cowboy."

I turned the music off for us to watch the sunset radiate on the glowing sandy redness. Soon the shadowy mesa structures lay under the stars.

"We're going to make love tonight, aren't we, Dalhart? We knew it even as we planned our excursion. Soul to soul and heartbeat to heartbeat stuff, though. That's what you had in mind. It's your style of laying claim to me. And it worked. I'm your woman. You're what I want."

****

"I got a feeling you're one of those guys that meditates, McIlhenny," Ira said as he lit up a cigar while driving down a dirt road. "You can roll down the window if the smoke gets to you, suck your ass."

"I meditate at night," I answered. "I have to put up with you and this job."

"I knew you probably did something weird like that. I bet you do yoga, too."

"No yoga."

"Listen, numbnuts. So what the hell you doing here? You don't fit. It's not that you're so damn stupid. You're the smartest guy I ever met, at everything but construction. You on some quest? Looking for your head?"

"I grew up on a farm. Later I worked computers in Houston, and it was the worst experience of my life. It was the fastest growing city in America, a thousand new families moving in every week. They all came for one reason. Money."

"So what the hell's wrong with that?" Ira defied. "That's why the unskilled come here and why the skilled go to Houston. You a back-to-nature freak? You like living in your van?"

"America's lost its soul," I complained.

"I knew it," he gruffed, blowing cigar smoke my direction. "What else they teach you in college?"

"My daddy was a war hero," I explained. "I got uncles that are preachers. I don't go to church much, but I got a lot on me. I joined the Marines to go to Vietnam. I need a cause, I guess. Now America's just one big party. So many in Houston were on drugs. New cars."

"A Texan needing an Alamo to defend." He laughed as he again blew smoke my direction.

"I don't like America anymore. Nothing for me

here."

"And so you're digging ditches in Gallup, New Mexico?" Ira smiled wickedly. "That makes sense. And you meditate to find your head? Smart people got too much time. Nothing else to do."

He pulled up to a big water pump. We looked to be in the exact center of nowhere. Nothing except miles of dirt.

"We're going to strip mine here pretty soon," he said as he pulled a shovel out of the back of the pickup. "I need you to dig a trough from this pump to those boxes over there." He pointed behind me at a stack of tomato boxes about fifty yards away. "You can meditate while you're doing it, doesn't bother me. Just dig straight. I'll be placing blasting caps in dynamite, so you might not want to get too close."

I was almost surprised he wasn't smoking on his cigar as he did so.

"This job sucks," I mumbled after a while, as I dug.

He looked up. "What did you say?"

"I hate this," I said sarcastically, straightening up and leaning on my shovel. "It's putting my chi at an imbalance. My harmony at a dysfunction."

"McIlhenny, shut up. People get fired for that. Whatever it is you said."

"Okay," I mumbled as I returned to my digging, "but this still sucks."

Ira went back to squeezing blasting caps with his pliers, then placed the sticks of dynamite in a box. He moseyed to the pickup, got a rope, made a loop, and began to twirl it. While I dug I suddenly felt the rope wrap around me, felt it jerk and tighten until it pulled me to the ground. Like some cowboy with a calf, Ira bent over me and tied up my hands and feet. He then got out a gasoline can from the pickup and, without blinking an eye, doused the bottom of my jeans and lit them with his cigarette lighter.

I felt the fire's warmth and pretended it hurt so he would get his stunt over with. It seemed to satisfy him, and he bent down, rolling me in the dirt until it was out.

"Now get back to work, McIlhenny," he grunted as he untied me. "Leave me to my danged blasting caps. Any other questions, queerbait?"

I kept a serious look on my face the rest of the afternoon, but found it hard to do so. This was fun. Maybe I brought all this on myself to break up the day.

"Quitting time, McIlhenny," I heard Ira shout.

"Another five minutes," I shouted back.

"I'll load up," he answered. "Oh yeah, another thing."

"What's that?" I asked when he didn't follow through.

"Didn't you say you used to play football?" he asked.

"Yeah."

"You're a fast runner, right?"

What does that mean? "Yeah," I answered again.

"You better be. This is a stick of dynamite here in my hand."

He lit it and threw it my direction. I didn't look back until I heard the explosion. There was a hole ten yards from where I used to be.

"Come on," he shouted again, not bothering to laugh. "Let's go home. Go get your shovel if it's still there."

Later I thought of Ira's shenanigans, sitting in the

restaurant, savoring the rich garlic aroma. He would have made a good Marine, I decided. I never made it to Vietnam, but I get to tell my grandkids about when I worked for the Kerr Construction Company.

I heard Carmen's voice come from beside me. "You got a look about you, *hombre*," she said as she walked over to me and planted a small kiss on my lips. "Is that a smirk? What wickedness are you contriving? Better not leave me out of it."

"Nearly got blown up by dynamite today," I said as my smirk turned into laughter.

"Good Lord, man. How did that happen?"

"Aw, not really," I said. "It's a long story anyway."

"Don't eat here tonight, Sweets," she said with a wink. "Mother has supper ready for us. She's going to bring up Monument Valley. She knows what the hell we did there. And I ain't talking the scenery or our intimate little conversations. I'm talking she put two and two together and she knows we're not virgins."

"She would've suspected what was going to happen even before we left."

"Yes," Carmen said with a grin, "but we've been so honorable that she felt she had to give us benefit of the doubt. But she was blunt when I got in last night. You coward, you knew it was coming, the way you dropped me off and hightailed it. So, I thought the best defense is a good offense and let her know how glorious it was. I added about classical music and our talks, for effect. I knew it wouldn't work, but it kept her busy for awhile."

"You admitted to her we made love?"

"You're telling me that an ex-Marine and a divorcee in their twenties don't know what they want

49

when the stars align? She knew it was going to happen. She just wants us to respect each other and not make it the centerfold of our relationship. Wait, centerfold, that's a pun, isn't it?" She laughed and gave another wink. "The centerpiece of our relationship. She adores you. You come over and exude virtue around her and she'll let it slide. She'll settle for just letting you know that she knows."

Carmen leaned over and planted a long, juicy kiss on me. I grabbed her as she readied to break away, pulled her back to me, and gave her one in return.

"Behave yourself," she said, feigning shyness. "The customers are looking. I hope so, anyway. Have a beer on me, *mi amour*," she said with a smile that sparkled. "Read your book and wait on me."

As she turned to walk away, she stopped, turned back, and embraced me. "I'm the happiest I've ever been. I'm one hundred percent your woman. I feel like brand new."

****

The crew was later than usual in leaving for the reservation the next day, as we gathered impatiently around the pickup. Finally the straggler we waited on appeared.

"Doug fired me," the Navajo worker said with contempt. "I gave my two weeks' notice, and he fired me on the spot. He said I wouldn't work hard now. Can you believe that son-of-a-bitch? I need the money. I'm going to Flagstaff."

"I could have told you," Jose said sympathetically. "I wish I knew you were quitting, and I would have warned you. That's his style."

"You wouldn't have told me nothing, Jose. You're

his boy. His lackey."

"I would have warned you," Jose replied sharply. "It's nothing to me to warn you. Can I help it if he likes me so much? Have I ever not helped anyone just because the boss man likes me?"

"Sorry, Jose. I'm just angry."

"I would be too," Jose sympathized. "I don't like Doug for this, and for other things, too. But he's good to me. I'm sorry, *amigo*."

This put a damper on our ride to the work site. But mostly I thought of Carmen and wore a thousand-mile stare as we rode.

"Hey, *gringo*," Jose said jokingly as he waved his hand in front of my face. "Come back to earth, man. Hey, we have a baptismal for my son at church on Sunday. I want you to come. Can you bring your camera?"

"Sure, Jose. I'd love to. It's only a Polaroid. My camera, I mean."

"Polaroid's great. Do you have any Sunday clothes? It's okay if you don't."

"I don't. I do have a shirt with a collar. A blue-jean shirt, though."

"I wanted you to be part of it," Jose said, "but you would need Sunday clothes. Just come. I would be honored."

I stared at Jose for a moment to see if he was finished about the baptism. He studied me. He could tell something was up.

"I met a girl, Jose," I blurted out finally.

"I knew it. To see your head in a cloud like this, I knew something happened."

"But she's Mexican."

"So's my wife, *gringo*."

I laughed. "I know. But I've got a problem."

"She's already pregnant?"

"I can't quit thinking about her."

Jose laughed and spoke Spanish to the others. "My thunderstruck *amigo* here," he said turning back to me. "Don't worry about it. You may be white, but you're a man. Men are disgusting. We'll go after anything."

"That's not it. She knocked my socks off. What am I going to do? If my mother found out, she would kill me. If my sister found out, she'd slit my throat. And the judge back home would consider it justifiable homicide."

More laughter throughout the pickup. "Oh, these *gringos* are son-of-a-bitches," Jose howled. "See, my mother is so much more open minded. She welcomed my wife even though she's Mexican. She even gave her blessing."

"I never liked a Mexican girl before," I said, hoping I sounded like a philosopher. "Anyone that wasn't white. And she's not even light-skinned like you. She's dark. I mean, let's go all the way. She was married to a white, though. At least that. I don't know how that matters, actually. I'm just clutching for straws."

I paid no mind to the laughter.

"My sister married a Yankee Catholic," I continued in my self-pity, "and my father almost disowned her. He apologized later, but…"

"What, you want to marry her or something, man?" Jose gasped. "I have to meet this girl."

"I don't want to marry her. But I can't get her off my mind. I wish we could go off to Alaska or something."

"Don't take this personal, Dalhart," Jose teased. "But you're such a *pendejo*."

****

Carmen watched me walk into the restaurant wearing a serious demeanor. I managed a smile, but it came out forced.

"Something happen at work?" she asked walking with me as I sought a table. "Dynamite? A fist fight? Did you just get fired?"

"Naw," I said before kissing her on the cheek.

"On the cheek? A kiss on the cheek? Hello, how are you, how's life? I get a kiss on the cheek? Dalhart, what's up with you today?"

"I finally told Jose about you," I explained.

"And?"

"You're more of me now."

"I repeat. And?"

"What are we going to do, Carmen?"

"About what?"

"About us."

"Let me think about that," she bit out. "Fall in love?"

I scoped her out. She stared darts into me.

Maybe it was because she was Hispanic, but she reminded me of a female Ricky Ricardo with her comical mannerisms.

"Let's see…" The heat of her anger was scorching. "I say in answer to your obnoxious question, the one about what are we going to do now that all your friends finally know about us after we've seen each other for a month, is, well, let's fall in love. And he just stands there. Listen, *cabron*, you better do some reassuring here real quick, or I'll kick you out of my mother's house before you ever get to move in."

"Carmen, I'm sorry. I'm not sure about what, but all I think about now is you and me. How happy we are. Now I've finally told everyone, and it makes it deeper somehow. This is getting serious."

"Dalhart—" The phrase is "if looks could kill." That's the kind of look Carmen shot at me now. "Ah. I don't know," she scoffed. "I was so happy until you walked in that door. Can we just start again before I knock you silly? How's your day, Sweetheart? And speaking of which, why haven't you told me yet that you love me? I've been dying to tell you, but you're the one passing through. I don't want to tie you down. But now it's starting to look like you don't want to be tied down." The right side of her upper lip curled in defiance. "I love you, Dalhart. There. Does that tie you down? To hell with you, then. I love you. We've been together for a month. We made love in Monument Valley. And we haven't since, for the record, but somehow it's gut-check time now. Say it to me or get the hell out of my restaurant." She turned to look at her boss, the owner. "Right?"

Her boss broke into laughter. "I can't help you out here, Dalhart, old buddy. You better fix this up."

"I love you, Carmen. Don't you get it? I love you. And I love loving you. That's what I hate about all this."

****

Moriah Energy was throwing a picnic for employees on Saturday. Kerr Construction was to set everything up, and we were invited because of it. More overtime pay.

"McIlhenny," someone called out. It was a gritty-looking guy I recognized. He drove heavy equipment. "Help me nail these two-by-fours for the stage we're building tomorrow."

He handed me a sledge hammer and placed a nail as large as a small spike on the end of one of the boards. I timidly tapped at the nail, hoping I wouldn't miss and break his hand. I'd never hit a nail with a sledge hammer before and thought I should warn him.

"Hit the damn thing, McIlhenny," he barked.

I struck at the nail a little harder.

"Damn it," he growled. "Hit the damn nail like you got some *huevos*."

He then grabbed the sledge hammer. "You hold this," he ordered, handing me the nail. "This is how you do it."

He reared back with the hammer well over his head, then swung with all his force. He drove perfect strikes the next three swings, driving the nail in.

"Here," he said handing the hammer back. "Now use a little gumption."

It was his funeral, I decided. I saw concern on his face as he watched the sledge hammer soar past the back of my head and then zero down on the nail he was holding. A perfect strike. I looked at him in celebration, happy for his still-intact hand. It was like the nail had a magnet on it. Three more swings and the nail went through the board and into the next one.

It was past ten at night as we piled into the back of the pickup to go home. Someone moaned that Doug's pickup approached, but I didn't care. I was disappointed I couldn't see Carmen at this hour.

"I need people at headquarters tomorrow morning

before we come up here," Doug yelped. "There's things to set up. Try to be there by eight. For those that can't make that, we're leaving for the celebration at ten-thirty or you get left."

He looked and saw me staring off into space.

"Did you hear me over there, McIlhenny?"

Jose nudged me. "Daddy's talking," he joked.

"McIlhenny, I need you at headquarters by eight tomorrow. Got that?"

"I'll be there," I answered.

He got out of his pickup, glaring at me the whole time as he walked toward us.

"We never did finish our little go-round from the other day, did we?" he said. I grimaced and looked the other way. "Get ready, McIlhenny. We're going to see what you're made of. It's overdue."

I sat stoically, still hoping he would go away. He didn't. He walked behind me, reached up, and grabbed me in a stranglehold, knocking off my hard hat. The fact that I wasn't in the mood got me all the angrier. The harder he put his arm in a lock around my neck, the more furious I became. Was I his little boy?

I jerked myself free from the headlock. The fact that I was so tall made it hard for him to hold on to my shirt collar. He grabbed at me and managed to bend me back down, but I grabbed him by the beard and then kicked upward toward his head. His hard hat flew off and the steel tip of my boot pounded into his temple, knocking him down.

"If you want a piece of me, step down," he growled.

I should have been mad, but I wasn't. He was off me, and that was enough.

"I don't want to fight you, Doug."

The calmness of my voice caught him off guard, and I saw the awkwardness on his face.

"I don't want to fight either," he said, seemingly ashamed, picking up his hard hat. "You're a good man," he said, getting into his pickup and driving off.

"Kick his ass," the rest of the crew said. Even Jose egged me on.

"He won't be any more trouble," I answered, and returned broodingly to my longings for Carmen.

It was nearly midnight when we got back to the headquarters of Kerr Construction Company. I got in my van and headed to the company area's exit. I turned the wheel right to go to my coworker's house for a shower, but before I stepped on the foot feed, I stared straight ahead. I had to see her. Even to renew our feelings. I turned the steering wheel toward the left and drove down the street.

I pounded on the door of her mother's house hard enough for someone to hear me, but not so hard as to irritate anyone. I hoped.

"Dalhart?" I heard Carmen say through the locked door. "Is it you?"

"Yes," I replied. "I have to get up early because we have extra work to do, but I need to see you. I need a kiss."

The door jerked open and she flew into my arms like in a Hollywood movie. Her body felt warm and light as a feather. In the shadows of nighttime I detected the black slip she wore, held on by its shoulder straps. There was no contrast with the black fabric on dark brown skin; the allure was strong with suggestiveness.

"I have to go," I said as we held onto each other.

"God, I don't want to go."

"Then stay, Dalhart. Mother will understand. She's got to understand. I can't take this. Come inside. Lay next to me."

"I can't do that, Carmen. How the hell am I not going to do that? But I can't do that."

I kissed her again, more forcefully and dramatically, for show and fun, than with the affection I felt. I then nudged her away and turned to walk back to my van with braggadocio. I took three steps, turned back to her, then ran to kiss her again.

"Someday I'm staying," I said, "but not tonight. Good night, *mi amour*."

Her form in the dark teased me. I couldn't take it. Is this God, or Mother Nature? But either way, I could not take it. I kissed her again with passion.

"I love you, Carmen. I—"

She reached up to stroke my hair. "What are we going to do?" she asked.

****

The daytime temperature in the desert of New Mexico reaches over a hundred. It's a dry heat that doesn't punish like the humidity back home, but it creates a constant thirst. I had not been getting enough water. During the night it got frigid. With my sleeping bag, I didn't get physically cold, but I was constantly breathing in cold air.

I was thirsty the entire night. When I awoke the next morning, I felt an irritation in my lungs and a raspiness in my throat. I tried ignoring it as I drove to work.

"You're the only one who showed up," Doug said angrily as I walked into the shed upon arriving. "I can't count on anyone for anything."

He led me to a roll of fence wire against the wall.

"We can manage this ourselves. The others can go to the picnic with Ira, if they ever show up. We have to load this and some tools into the pickup. The poles are already there. We have to partition off an area."

He complained the whole trip about how no one worked hard and no one was loyal except me. I thought about telling him why, but decided it wasn't the time.

Doug and I were still building the fence when some of the management from Moriah Energy began addressing the miners. After the speeches, the miners formed into groups for competitions, and the Kerr group formed into one of its own. We won the tug of war, and Ira won the hammer-strong-man event of high target.

Next was a fifty-yard dash. Those entering were cocky, and I wondered why. I had been up most of the night, had gotten up early to work, and was in my work clothes, including steel-toed boots. But so what?

"Where you going, McIlhenny?" Ira asked.

"I can beat these turkeys," I boasted.

"What makes you so sure of yourself? Because you're an ex-Marine?"

"Yeah, and I used to play football."

"So did some of them."

"But I'm from Texas."

I was in front the whole time and won by five yards.

"You lucked out," Ira scoffed as I returned.

"You make your own luck, Ira."

"You got a saying for everything, don't you?"

"That's what they're there for." I smirked.

Even after supper I felt drained. I purposely avoided Carmen's restaurant and ate pizza. I needed to conserve my energy for when I had her alone. I was limp as I ate, and could barely keep my head up.

"I was afraid you worked late again," Carmen said as a greeting at the door to her mother's house. She leaned up to kiss me, but my kiss back was limp. "What's wrong?" she asked. "Come on in. Let's sit on the couch."

"I don't know if it's my glands," I said. "They don't feel swollen, but they're irritated. It may be my sinuses. I don't have a runny nose, but maybe it's a cold just starting."

"Oh, Dalhart, what will you do? You're a laborer. You don't get time off. Not paid leave, anyway. Tomorrow's Sunday. Stay with me. Take it easy. You'll be okay."

She held me by the hand and led me to the couch in the living room. She sat down at one end and gently tugged at me to lie down and place my head on her lap.

"I got sick at Camp Pendleton both times I was there, in the Marines," I reminisced to her. "I think the same thing is happening now."

"Oh, no." Carmen sighed as she rubbed my cheek gently with one hand and stroked my hair with the other. "You just got into my life. I can't bear you to feel so much stress. What will happen now? What will you do? What will I do?"

She struggled to lean down but managed to kiss my forehead. I lay like a wet dishrag, taking in all the energy she was prepared to give me.

"If I fall asleep," I whispered, "I'm sorry."

"No, no, no," she pleaded. "Oh, Dalhart, no. Don't

let anything be wrong. And we were so patient and honorable with each other, and now, what if we never get to give ourselves to each other again? I don't mean to sound selfish."

I slowly and painfully raised my hand to touch her forearm as she stroked more of my hair.

"It was important, Carmen," I said listlessly. "I needed to go slowly. I needed to get to know you, but mostly I needed for you to know me more. I'm different, Carmen. Different from anyone you've ever met. I cherish the time we made love, but this had to be real. Beyond sense gratification. Beyond whim."

"Yes, you are so different, Dalhart. You're special. But you give me so little credit that I understand how you feel about it, about us going slowly with one another. I've been understanding. Please accept I have."

"I've had flings before, Carmen. I've enjoyed myself at a girl's expense before. Your mother was right to make us promise. I probably would have pounced on you if she hadn't made us promise. You're so pretty and full of life. You have a spark. I can't resist. All that is good. But I wanted more from you. And from myself. Beyond this sense gratification thing, like I said. All that's okay. Nature has its way. This replenish-the-earth thing. All these biological instructions going on inside us. But there's more to us than that, and you get trapped by it so easily. It takes on a life of its own. That's why so many religions try to discipline it out of you. I don't agree with that. But I understand it. But all these demands of Mother Nature are fulfilling, too, even spiritually. But not if it's just another reason to party."

"Dalhart." She grinned. "Are you delirious? You're

such a philosopher. Please, just get well. You're rambling on like you have to tell your life story in the next five minutes."

"Can you handle it?" I asked fearfully. "It's so hungry inside, Carmen. I don't know if I can make you happy. Other girls have wanted things from me. It gets old. I'm not trying to sound trite, but it gets so shallow. I need more. In Houston they were throwing themselves at me. I didn't think a person could get bored with sex. But I didn't want anyone after awhile."

"It's okay, Dalhart. Relax. I understand. It's all right, *mi amour*. I told you about my marriage. I understand what you're saying. I love that you're different. Don't worry. Just get well, sweetheart. Relax, darling."

"What if you reject me and want the party stuff?" I whined. "I need answers in my life. But I don't even know the questions yet. I'll drive you crazy. You'll reject me."

"Me reject you? You are crazy. You're the most exciting person I've ever met."

I reached up to feel her cheek. "Others have thought so too," I explained. "Until they find out. I'm so complicated. I'm so vulnerable, Carmen. You'll reject me if all you want from me is a good time."

She touched my lips with her fingertips. "Shhh," she said. "You're sick and feeling insecure. I'm here. There's more to me than a good time. You haven't seen that yet? Dalhart, you're hurting me that you don't see how I love what we've been. I know you're sick and insecure, but please, know who I am. Know what you've made me. Sleep, sweetheart. Stay here all night. You're home now. With me. Neither of us has anything. Suddenly, with you in my life, it's like I have everything. Pow, just like that. So go to sleep, Dalhart. Feel my warmth."

I could barely breathe all night and felt weak the next morning. I was glad it was Sunday, but I had to go to Jose's baptismal. My throat hurt, but mostly it was my lungs. I felt congested.

Carmen was up by the time I got dressed for Jose's ceremony. She prepared breakfast.

"Mother saw us on the couch last night," Carmen said as I sat down at the dining table in the kitchen. "It's okay. You're family now to her. She adores you. I explained you were sick, and she kissed you on the cheek and left us. You were snoring. You were so out of it. I wanted to carry you to my bed, but I slept well on the couch even slouched like I was. Our first night together. Well, not counting Monument Valley, of course."

I smiled at the thought but then turned serious again. "I can't afford to be sick, and I don't have insurance, except through Kerr for injuries incurred on the job. Nothing for illness. If your mother doesn't mind, I'll sleep on her couch. Maybe I'll get over whatever I have, with rest and a warm bed, meaning the couch. We're not sleeping together while we're at your mom's. I have to respect her. But I do need a warm bed, if it's not imposing. I have to go to a baby christening now, but I'll be back by noon."

"You don't look good, *amigo*," Jose said when I showed up at the church.

"I'm scared I can't go to work tomorrow. Maybe even for a few days. Doug's going to fire me."

"He won't fire you," Jose assured. "He likes you.

63

Thanks for coming. And thanks for bringing your Polaroid. I want to remember this day."

****

I made it through three work days. After each day I went to what now felt like home. Carmen's mother babied me until her daughter came home from work. Then Carmen took over while her mother trustingly left us to ourselves. Carmen laid out a mattress on the floor next to the couch, to sleep next to me.

I could not get up on the fourth day of my illness. That afternoon I drove to the Kerr offices and told old man Kerr I was too sick to go on. I would return to Texas.

"I'll never see you again," Carmen said, bravely as much as bitterly, when I told her of my plans. "You'll forget us hicks in Gallup, New Mexico. If you're going to stay at your mom's anyway, until you recover, I don't see why you can't stay here. A mother's a mother. I come attached with mine."

"I've imposed long enough," I replied. "I don't know how long this will take."

"It's no imposition," Carmen pleaded. "You heard my mother tell you this."

"But then it becomes one."

"And then what?" she asked. "What will you do then? In your post-Carmen world?"

"I have your address and your phone number," I said hoping it would reconcile her to my departure.

"Ahh," she scoffed. "You're brushing me off. You may not know it, but that's what you're doing. You're not even well enough to drive that far, but you're still leaving me."

I stood silently. I wanted so much to convince her,

but I didn't think I could. I even wondered if she wasn't right. Out of sight, out of mind. Gallup might seem like halfway around the world by the time I recovered. But it was time to leave. Time to find out about the rest of my life and if she would be a part of it.

New Mexico looked even prettier on the drive back. And now it was a part of me.

****

"I remember when you came home from boot camp," my mother said as she brought soup into my bedroom and set it next to my bed. "You were so gaunt then, sunken cheeks, and so pale. I'd hear you coughing all night, those dry coughs. You were on the verge of pneumonia. Now too, I think."

"I guess that medicine is helping, though," I said. "I couldn't afford a doctor, but a pharmacist recommended something when I told her my problem. I can't afford pneumonia."

"You just need some rest," Mother assured. "You'd be coming home in a couple of weeks anyway. School starts soon."

"I didn't save enough money. I don't know if I can pay tuition and have what I need to live on, besides."

"You've still got the G.I. bill," she reminded, "and you're a grad assistant. Did you get enough material for your thesis?"

"I could write a novel."

"Write your thesis first."

"I got sick and came home to my mommy," I mocked. "Jose can't do that. And he has to worry about being deported, too."

"You lived in an old panel truck," she summarized. "You weren't insured, you survived on minimum wage

65

and saved money for school too. All for a thesis. You don't do anything the easy way. You can't stay in summer school like the others and do research in a library. You have to go out in the desert with a bunch of illegals and Navajos. Collecting primary data, you call it. Always living on the edge is what it is. You'll never change. You joined the Marines in the middle of a war nobody else wanted to fight. Don't you need security, like a normal person?"

"Security is boring," I answered, trying to feel brave again. "But—"

"But what?"

"Mother, I need to tell you something. You're not going to like it."

"You're gay?" She looked harshly at me. "That's why, in spite of all those girls throwing themselves at you, you never got married?"

"Worse than that. I'm in love with a Mexican."

"Male or female?"

"Female, Mother. Get real."

"Just thought I'd ask." She sighed in relief. "Everyone else you grew up with is on their second marriage now, and you go traipsing off into the desert. You may not be gay, but you're weird. So, what do you mean, you fell in love with a Mexican girl?"

"I met her after I started work in Gallup, a couple of weeks later. It got deep. Real, real deep. Then when I got sick, she and her mom helped keep me alive. Except for her brown skin, you'd love her. She's poor, though. But she's got class, and her mom is an angel."

"What do you mean, if it weren't for her brown skin? You act like I'm a racist or something. Did you tell her that? Just how serious are you? In love, I know.

How much in love?"

"Totally, incredibly in love."

"From just over a month? Are you sure?"

"I found the love of my life from knowing her just over a month. And not only that, one of the greatest friends I've ever had and admired is an illegal from Durango, Mexico. I'm going to miss them. I hate it."

"You'd have brown-skinned kids, wouldn't you? If you pursue this relationship with this Mexican girl. I'd have brown-skinned grandkids." She sat back as a smile eased onto her face. "I'm part Cherokee, after all. I have olive skin. Remember when I'd get sun, and then we'd go across the border and the border patrol wouldn't let me back in Texas until I could prove I was American? God plays his little games, doesn't he? So now I'm warming up to her like he planned it or something. When can I meet this girl? Is she going to be my daughter-in-law?"

"I don't know if she'll be your daughter-in-law. I'm going to see if I can forget her. Then I'll know."

"Here we go again," my mother complained. "My son just can't settle down. I finally got me a daughter-in-law and grandkids, and I can't even meet them because they won't exist."

****

The cough persisted until after classes began, and I wasn't able to jog or lift weights for a month.

One night I dreamed of Jose. I don't know if it was something I read in my research that stirred it, but the dream haunted. How he called out to me. "Don't forget me," he pleaded in the dream. People like him need to know there's a Dalhart McIlhenny in the world.

And I never forgot Carmen.

"Hello," I heard her mother say. "Hello. Who is this calling, please?"

My heart swooned to hear her voice. I wanted to talk to her.

"Hey, this is Dalhart McIlhenny," I said, my voice edged with the excitement of being in touch with them again. "Is Carmen available?"

"Dalhart? This is Dalhart? Oh, Dalhart, are you all right? We were so worried about you this whole time. It's been over a month, Dalhart. You broke my baby's heart. We didn't know if you were okay. You were so sick when you left us, and then we didn't hear diddly squat. Not even one call from you. Carmen, my poor, poor baby, has been frantic."

I had to control myself to keep from choking up. I felt terrible. I'd been so preoccupied with getting well and sorting out my life, I left her hanging. I had barely considered that. I understood why. I didn't want to light any candles of waiting and want. But suddenly I felt so selfish and wondered why it had taken so long to feel the need to call her.

"Carmen," I heard her mother yell out, with the phone obviously away from her mouth. "Carmen, dear, it's Dalhart. Come, baby. He's calling from— Wait a minute." I heard a breath into the receiver and knew her mother must be ready to talk again to me. "Dalhart, are you in Gallup? You know where we live, though. Where are you calling from?"

"Texas," I answered.

"Are you still at your mom's?"

"No, ma'am. I'm at Texas A&M."

"Texas A&M? Isn't that where you went to college?"

"Yes, ma'am."

"Let me speak to him, Mother," I heard Carmen's voice say in the background.

"Here she is, Dalhart."

"Dalhart. Is this really you?" Carmen asked.

"Yes, it is, Carmen. I'm so sorry I didn't call. I love you, Carmen. Please forgive me for not calling until now."

"Is it true? You're at your college?"

"Yes, it is, *mi amour*. I have so much to say to you."

"Is that good?" she fretted.

"It's up to you if it is. I miss you. I want you to come live with me. I want to spend the rest of my life with you. Do you think that might happen?"

"I don't know what to say to you, Dalhart. I can't believe how you just left me hanging. Now you call and somehow at the snap of your fingers I'm supposed to run off to Texas with you? I've lived that life before. No, thanks."

"I know. Can we talk? Can we talk for the rest of our lives? I was sick, and I told my mother about you and she wants me to marry you, and I had to know if it was the right thing to do."

"How could you not know that? How could you not know that, Dalhart? What did I not do that you don't know that by now? You hurt me. You hurt me. I wanted to hurt you back, but you didn't care enough about me to hurt. Why did you call now? Why all of a sudden now? I'm married."

The silence was deafening.

"No, I'm not, *cabron*," she finally said, "but I should be. I haven't even seen anyone, and I should have been dating every truck driver passing through here. Did I call you *cabron*? I don't want to see you."

"Do anyhow. I don't deserve it, but do it anyhow. I want to marry you. I want you to come here to Texas and marry me."

"Why should I come to you?"

"Because I don't deserve it. But I'm in school again. I can't come out there. I didn't only just now graduate like I told everyone in Gallup. I'm actually finishing up my master's degree and soon will start my doctorate. I live in an old wooden shack made in World War I. It's south of the Texas A&M campus. It has a dining room that's part of the living room, a bathroom, and two bedrooms. I have a mattress on the floor that would be so cozy to share with you. Do it. Share it and my life."

I heard her chuckle. "*Pendejo*. My God. Yes, I'll marry you, Dalhart. Of course, I will. That's exactly what I want with my life. To spend it with you. I love you, Dalhart. I love you so much. You hurt me so badly. I can't believe you waited for over a month to get hold of me. You were so unsure of yourself while you were here in Gallup. You sound like you know what you want now. I love that it's me."

"It is, Carmen. I've never been so sure of anything."

"Then it was worth the wait and the hurt," she replied. "I think you're stupid, but I sort of understand."

"I talked it over with my mother," I explained. "She and my sister are going to drive out there to pick you up. Bring whatever you need. For sure bring your birth certificate. We'll get married as soon as we can. We'll settle in, find you a job, get the license, and live happily ever after."

"Can I find work out there?"

"Of course, you can, silly. I can't support you anyway. I need you to help support me. How's that? You'll be the money winner. I get by, but barely, and have to pay for college too. So, ha."

"So, then, I'll make all the decisions. Wear the pants in the family."

"As long as we're family," I said in as corny a way as I could.

"Yeah, *mi amour*," she answered, "as long as we're family."

"I sold Desperado," I moaned. "I needed the money, especially after getting sick. I have a two-door sedan though. I already had it. I just didn't bring it to Gallup because I couldn't live in it."

"Desperado was ours," she said pouting. "We made love in it for the first time. It should be a museum."

"I know," I sighed. "Don't make me feel worse. But you can have the car. I get around on a bicycle."

"We can't make love on a bicycle, silly boy."

"Carmen, before you come out, go by Kerr Construction and tell Jose all this. Tell everybody. Doug and Ira too. I never introduced you to them. Tell them they're invited to the wedding. They ain't gonna come to it, they're too busy and it's too far, but make them pretend they will."

"I don't know any of these guys," she said.

"Just go to Kerr Construction and find Doug. Ask for Jose and Ira too. It's important."

I loved the thought of my mother and sister making the same drive I had made at the beginning of the summer. A summer that changed my life.

The three of them got to know each other on the ride back from Gallup. Carmen spent the night with them in a motel, her first night in College Station. I had a mattress in the guest bedroom of my shack, but it wasn't big enough for all three of them. Everyone knew where she was going to sleep when they left, but we cherished the games one must play to respect family.

"A picture of Monument Valley," Carmen noted as she entered my shack for the first time.

"I found this poster when I was buying a textbook I needed," I explained. "Can you believe? Made to order. I tacked it on the wall in our living room here as our major artwork. It was the last straw, actually. I pined over you every day, but when I saw this poster is when I finally broke down and called you up. And asked you to marry me."

She walked over to the poster and gave it a kiss.

"That weekend in Monument Valley was our honeymoon, you know," she said while staring at the poster nostalgically.

I nodded. "And now we have the rest of our lives," I said.

****

I look back at what I consider the best summer of my life. And it led directly to a wonderful life with Carmen and our three boys. I'm a tenured professor now. I've written books and articles from my case studies. I have possessions and comforts. I haven't saved the world, not that I ever meant to. But I have my memories. And I know the people from these memories are the ones who taught me the most.

Rendezvous with Fay

The ache inside over Monica stayed with me every mile that I drove from Los Angeles to San Diego. Driving past Camp Pendleton took some of the edge off momentarily as I recalled my proud past, my days in the Marine Corps. Soon, however, the frustrations of that time during the so-called Age of Aquarius made the anger and pain inside me even more pronounced. That conflict, in fact, the Aquarian versus the Spartan back in the early 1970s, was a perfect match for the conflict these few years later with her.

Why I had gotten mixed up with a hippie was beyond me. And as much as I hated the anguish inside, I relished it, too. Emotional self-flagellation—I deserved every ounce. Teach me what I need and let me move on with my life. The sooner the better. Amen.

As I entered the outskirts of San Diego, warm memories predominated once more. My days as a private in the United States Marine Corps had begun here. Cherished days. Sacred days. Defiant days, as I joined to go to Vietnam and to take a patriotic stand. A stand against people like Monica, in fact, even though I hadn't met her yet.

The defiance coming out now about those precious days was welcomed by me. I liked the grit and the fight in me again and preferred it over the hurt and moping I had been feeling while trying to work things out with her the last few weeks. At least I knew I'd tried with her, but the defiance now gave me new wings and new direction.

I haphazardly checked the map as I drove on the freeway. Fay lived near the Chula Vista area just off the freeway I was on. I had her address scribbled on the map in big bold letters, as if she was someone of importance, which she was, with a huge X to mark the area of San Diego where that address was located.

More and more, as I drove, thoughts of Fay and our days in Frankfurt, West Germany, barely two years before, prevailed. I regretted not knowing her better. I even resented that I didn't. I was with Monica then, while Fay was with her boyfriend Joe. Me, the one Texan, trying to mix with these damn Californians. Except Fay was not damned. Anything but. And she didn't belong in California, I determined, even back then. She had much the makings of a perfect southern belle.

And that's why I was in San Diego.

The address was of a nice, middle-class apartment complex. It lay in a prosperous-looking neighborhood. Was Fay well off? She was a keypunch operator back in Frankfurt, on the US Air Force base where we worked in 1974, and from her letters I understood she was doing something like that in San Diego. That and secretarial work. I doubted that paid very much even in San Diego.

I searched for the wing of the complex that held her apartment number. My mood was still sullen, but the closer I got to her apartment, the more I began to perk up. As I walked by the swimming pool area, suddenly I heard my name called out.

"Dutch!" someone yelled.

I turned toward the chairs at the side of the pool,

where people were sunbathing. A tall, slim, tanned, gorgeous, bikini-clad body ran toward me. She had her long brown hair in a ponytail that swung as she ran.

"Dutch," she yelled again as she hugged me. "It's so good to see you. I can't believe how excited I am! Someone from back then, the not-so-old days in Frankfurt."

Before I got to hug her in return, she pulled away to grab my hand and lead me out of the pool area. As we walked, she gave a jump-skip for a step in glee while she swung my hand with hers joyously.

"You let your hair grow out again," she commented as we walked. "I like it. To the nape of your neck like when Joe and I first met you back then, before you cut it all off. You look good. It's so blond. Just like the surfer boys here. Except you have a long, tall, husky Texas body. And I'm sure you still have your washboard abs. I like that even better. I remember the first time I watched you work out in the gym and saw that washboard stomach of yours. I was so shocked. 'This guy is a Marine from Texas,' I thought to myself back then."

As friendly as Fay's demeanor always seemed to be, and as warm as the memories were, I was surprised at the celebration she exhibited in our reunion. Any regret I ever had back then in Frankfurt about not pursuing her, about any longing inside toward her, magnified in me as we walked to her apartment. *What did I leave behind there in Germany? And why the hell did I leave it?* I thought as she left me to myself while she changed her clothes.

"I see you changed into something more comfortable," I joked sarcastically as Fay re-entered her living room wearing a light blue jumper outfit.

"I know." She laughed in return. "But for chumming around in the living room, this actually is more comfortable. Just not to your eyes, maybe. Anyway, listen, Dutch, I'd love to make you some coffee, but maybe you'd like to go out and have some refreshment in a restaurant. Or even a beer? What ya like, bro?"

"It's cozy here, Fay. Let's just have coffee here and chat. Catch up on old times. Or not-so-old times, as you said before."

"That works for me," she answered. "Give me a minute and I'll put the coffee on. Would you prefer brewed or instant?"

"Doesn't matter. What you want?"

"I prefer brewed. I'll just put it on and come back out."

She walked to the other side of the living room before turning to say more.

"My mom would like to meet you. We'll venture out to her place later this afternoon. You'll love my mom."

I smiled to be polite but was sure I would indeed like her mom, just seeing how Fay had turned out in her life.

"Coffee'll be ready in about five minutes," Fay said as she returned to sit in an armchair in front of me. "So, listen, how did it go with Monica, if you don't mind my asking?"

"Just now, you mean? My visit now with her? Or when she came back to California after we left Frankfurt?"

"All the above, I suppose," Fay said cautiously.

"Start wherever you like. I know it was all difficult for you, and we haven't talked much about it. It was nice that we've been writing, and I didn't want to intrude on you to spoil things by asking your status. I'd like to know whatever you feel you can talk about. I adore both of you, so it's more than just curiosity. But once again, I don't want to intrude on anything very personal for you."

"To be honest, Fay, there's no one I'd rather talk about it with than you. And I have a lot to get off my chest, so I hope I don't make you regret you asked."

"No way. I really want to know, and I really care about the both of you. You both were just the greatest hosts to me and Joe when we first arrived there in Frankfurt, and then friends to us afterwards when we got our jobs and all. Actually, Joe never did get a job. And Joe and I never did get an apartment so we kept using your shower the whole time while we slept in Joe's Volkswagen van."

"Aha," I chirped at the memory. "That VW van of yours."

She let out a laugh. "But let's don't get into that yet," she said. "Those days we were all together in Frankfurt, I mean. Tell me how things were for you two after you left Frankfurt back in 1974. And on to now, two years later. Or start with now. Whatever. But wait—I'm sure the coffee is ready. I'll be right back. How do you want your coffee, by the way?"

"A bit of cream, and also I prefer honey to sugar, if you have any."

"Honey? Wow. I never heard of anyone using honey. I have some, though. I'll just bring the cream and honey out, and you can fix it yourself. Give me a second."

And where was I going to start in this soap opera about Monica and myself? And how much was I going to say? But I could feel the urgency to get things out about all of it.

Dutifully, Fay returned, her hands filled with a large tray containing the coffeepot, a small pitcher of cream, some sugar cubes, and a small jar of honey. She placed them on the coffee table between us without looking up at me until she seated herself.

"Help yourself," she offered.

"Do you know what happened between Monica and me after we left Frankfurt?" I asked Fay while we stirred at our cups of coffee.

"Just what you told me in letters after you got back to Texas. What little you told me, I might add. Monica didn't say much either. And you and I are both still in contact with our friend Eva there, that we met at the Air Force base in Frankfurt. She and her husband are in Kansas City now, at an Air Force base, as you know. We've been writing and sharing information. You didn't tell either one of us very much. So, again, start where you like."

I took a deep breath, as much for dramatic effect as to ponder through the maze of where to begin.

"I'll just touch on our last days in Frankfurt and when we returned to America. Just to get the setting. Then skip over until now. Now is what's really pressing me. I need to talk about that the most."

Fay grimaced at my introduction. It was my warning to her. This was going to be deep. I thought for a moment and decided I should lighten the setting up a bit first.

"Since you mentioned Eva, do you remember how I first met her back then? It was just before you and Joe arrived on the scene."

"If you told me the story, I don't remember."

"Monica and I lived five miles from the base, as you well know. We had to walk every day through that forest just outside the base, to get to work and back from our little studio apartment. Or to shop at the PX, or to see a movie, or whatever we did on base."

Fay smiled as I brought back the scene.

"Joe and I never could give you two a ride," she said. "Joe never found work, and my job shift was different from yours, so it never worked out. You did so much for us, and we couldn't even give you a lift to the base."

"Makes for a better story, though," I said, reminiscing. "Us on foot everywhere. Makes us sound like pioneers. Anyway, one day Monica and I left the PX with a bag of groceries each. You know, American stuff we couldn't get on the Frankfurt economy. We were just leaving the base and heading toward the forest to start our five-mile walk when this car stopped. It was Eva and her husband. Eva rolled down the window, and in the biggest Southern accent in history, she asked us if we needed a lift. The thoughtfulness and that accent melted me through the floor. Monica too. We crawled into the back seat of their car and started getting to know each other. Next thing you know, Eva is my best friend. She finally found a fellow hick."

"You are not a hick, Dutch. The proudest Southerner I ever met, for sure. Eva's accent, though, is a doozy. It had to bring out whatever cultural genetics abounded in you."

"It did indeed do that. I was so homesick after talking to her I was ready to jump out of my skin. We got onto food and recipes, and the next thing you know she invites Monica and me over to their house on the base and had us turning a one-eighty there on the highway, taking us back to the base to make a pot of chili. Home-cooked chili for a Texas boy, me, and Southern hospitality, too, and later on, country music. I thought I was going to OD. Monica melted all the more. Those were good days for us. After all Monica's arrogance about Neanderthals from the South, then to be taken in by me, and then by Eva, her head was swimming in confusion about all of her supposed 'hip' California values."

It got silent after that memory, as my present depressing situation came back to mind. I turned my head away solemnly to adjust.

"They were good days for sure, Dutch." Fay obviously hoped to lighten me up again. "For you and Monica, which is about the time we all met. And for Joe and me, too. Not just to be hosted by you and how you helped me find a job, but also how Eva provided the home touch for Joe and me too. Really warm, wonderful days to remember."

"Anyway, that's why you and Eva have heard anything at all about us lately," I continued with my story. "Monica and I both trusted y'all more than anyone and so told you things."

Fay smiled appreciatively and waited for me to continue. I looked her directly in the eyes and fought for the strength to begin.

As if to rescue us from this drama, the telephone rang. Fay bounced up from her chair and walked to the wall phone a few feet behind her.

"Yes, Mother, he's here. I could not believe how great it is to see him."

Fay listened for a moment to the other end of the conversation.

"We were having coffee. He only just got here."

Fay listened further.

"Sure, no problem," Fay said into the phone. "We'll bring our coffee with us, so don't worry about serving us anything. We're leaving now."

Fay hung up the phone and looked at me.

"I guess you heard, dude," she chirped. "That was my mother, and she is dying to meet this guy from my exotic past. We'll talk about you and Monica on the way. Bring your coffee and whatever else."

Fay walked back toward me, picked up her cup of coffee, then motioned me with her other hand to follow before locking the door to her apartment. She grabbed my hand to hold affectionately as we walked. I was glad. It perked me right up from the dramatic mindset I had entered while picturing my time with Monica.

"You'll love San Diego, Dutch," she said as we drove along. "I know I'm prejudiced, since this is my hometown and all, but this is a wonderful place. I wish you had more time to stay. There's so much to show you." She looked at me with her broad smile. "Starting with my mom's. You'll love my mother."

I smiled back. I still needed to talk about Monica, but now I wished I didn't have to. I loved how cheerful Fay could make me in just a flash.

"Okay, it'll be a few minutes before we get to my mom's. Talk to me some more about Monica. Do you remember where you were?"

I nodded.

"We hadn't really gotten into it yet about our problems. I was just starting."

"I'm all ears, Dutch. Lay it on me. I'm ready."

Feeling much refreshed now, so was I.

"It wasn't Monica who changed during our relationship," I began. "It was me. Y'all saw us happy in the beginning, but then came the turmoil. I went through a transition."

I saw a confused look as Fay patiently waited for the explanation while she drove.

"Monica was precious," I continued. "So precious. I remember when we first met. I was working at that base gas station, in the beginning. I was on my way to the canteen for lunch, and half way there I met these two girls in military jackets and blue jeans. Both had backpacks. They came up to me and pretty much blocked my path on the sidewalk. One of them—you never met her; she was gone by the time you and Joe met me—asked me if I was from Texas. I told her I was, so she said I had been pointed out by some of the airmen. Somehow people knew who I was and how I seemed to be a survivor. So this girl kept asking me questions about how to find work on base, and so on. This girl would ask a question, but I was already enraptured by her companion, Monica. Monica had this charisma, this persona, and was all shy and feeling vulnerable. They had just flown to Luxembourg from California, by way of New York, and had fifty dollars to their name. So I'm talking to this girl about all of their circumstances, and looking at Monica instead while I did so. It embarrassed me how I was so stupid about it. Crazy. But I was so captured and charmed by

Monica before she ever opened her mouth."

"She certainly had charm, Dutch. She was so sensitive and deep."

"You know the story about how I put her up—or, actually, *them* up—and helped them find work as chambermaids in the base hotel. So I'll move on now to where I changed later on, after Monica and I fell in love with one another. I have to pass up a lot of endearing and wonderful days Monica and I had, and the bad will come out of context, which is unfair to her. But you've seen the good in her, so that'll help give you some perspective."

"You two were very happy when you took Joe and me in. And thank God you got that job at the gas station before you started working for the civil service later, or Joe and I would never have found you. We just arrived, like we were fated to meet you, at that gas station. As if you were there for us, and you offered to help us out while you were pumping gas for us. Very endearing memories of you, Dutch."

"Yes, good memories," I said, smiling as I recalled the scene. "And I'm glad you saw all of that with Monica and me in our good times, so you know how it was. I hate leaving it out, but at least you saw it. I need to cut to the problems and why all this affected me so much. Monica had this other side, this dark bitter side. She hated everything—Nixon, the military, Southerners, the rich, and the war, of course. Mostly she hated people. She hated everyone. Not quite literally, I know."

"Except that she loved you, Dutch. She was so in love with you. The one thing she loved was you."

My throat tightened, and I felt my eyes moisten. In

desperation I rolled my eyes, hoping to spread the forming tears before they could trickle down my cheek. I turned away from Fay, hoping to regain my composure. She instinctively raised her right hand from the steering wheel toward me as if ready to comfort me, but then pulled back as if not wanting to interfere with my struggle.

I gritted my teeth angrily, trying to snap out of my remorse. Finally, I was calm again and turned back toward Fay.

"The one thing she loved was me," I acknowledged. "And I failed her. I knew I failed her. I was so in love with her, but every day I heard all this vitriol about every facet of life. The sellouts, the cheats, the scammers, the phonies, the idiots, the pigs. It got to me. It was like she was born on the wrong side of the bed. I kept hoping I could make a difference in her in all of that. But I guess where I really cracked about it was when my father wrote me. He asked me to come home and take over the family farm. I was happy in Europe. I was happy with Monica. I didn't want to go back home. But I wanted to make my dad happy, and also I felt I belonged back on the farm. America was changing. Maybe I could hold on to some of the America that raised me by going back to the farm with my dad."

"So how did that matter then with Monica? You didn't want to leave her?"

"Things were coming to a head with her anyway, but I had to make a decision. I asked Monica to marry me and come with me to the farm. She swooned when I asked her to marry me. It touched me. This girl really wanted to marry me. But she shuddered at the thought of going to Hicksville, Texas. And that's when I started changing. Until then I could hope for the best, hope that I could make a difference in her outlooks. I was even challenged by the thought that we could work out things about life, with time. But now everything was staring me in the face. I had to take this attitude of hers about everything seriously. All of her. Not just being in love and hoping maybe in time her demeanor would get better."

Fay nodded her head as if she followed how I felt. I saw her ready to comment, but then she waited for me to continue.

"Part of Monica liked the idea of living on a farm and getting back to nature, sort of. But I could see her hating my father someday, and my friends, my hometown, everything. She would never have fit. If we could have just gone off after Frankfurt and travelled around Europe or wherever, lived day to day and gone on from there, who knows what would have happened. But now I felt stuck with a situation I didn't think I could handle, and one Monica would never handle."

"Did you stop loving her?" Fay asked.

"I still loved her. I even felt it. Love for her. Caring about her. I just felt so stuck with the rest of the story about her."

"That makes sense," Fay said sympathetically. "So it went down from there."

"It went the hell down from there. I started being irritable, and picky with her, and impatient. I started making her cry. I hated seeing her cry, but then made her cry more, wanting her so badly on the one hand and feeling so stuck on the other."

"I remember you spent a month by yourself," Fay

recalled, "after Monica went back home to California. How you talked to me about getting married to her, but she needed to go home first and see her family and think. What did that mean? Why go home to think? It's a serious step to get married, so you *should* think about it. But she went back home and left you here. So I was never sure of your status together. I guess none of us were supposed to know."

"Monica and I talked about getting married even as she left. We were hoping time apart would help clear things for us. It sort of did. She rejected me after I got home from travelling Europe. Any thought of marriage was off the books. I was told as much, right off, when I called her from JFK airport in New York after I arrived back. I was relieved but frustrated. And I had a horrible guilt complex, except I was sure we'd have never made it."

"You wouldn't have, Dutch. I'm not trying to ease any guilt you feel. I understand all of that. But you two weren't going to make it. You were so opposite, except that you loved each other, and you both have that sensitivity. This is not just me saying this. Eva thought so too. So did Joe. It was complex, but you just weren't going to make it."

"I don't know if that makes me feel better, but I at least don't feel worse."

"And so why did you leave your job in Houston this year and go to Los Angeles to see her this spring? Eva and I were confused, but again, there is so much we don't know."

"Monica was so bitter. And she just stayed bitter the whole time I was with her in L.A. I still loved her, but also I was disgusted with her, with her eternal bitterness. She is bitter about everything, and the fiasco with me just made it more so. Part of me felt like I owed her and had unfinished business with her. It haunted me how she loved me. I had a chance to help her somehow, or so I hoped. And when she began to hate me while I was with her in L.A., it enraged me. Ha! The audacity! I know everybody thinks that way, that somehow they can change people for the better and how dare the other person not change. But I felt I might help her outlook on life, on finding herself. Help her not take the worst possible view about everything. We really loved each other, and the talks we had before I left Houston to see her made me feel like we should try."

"It's noble," Fay commented. "It's so Southern, and Marine, too, wanting to make a difference. But Eva and I knew you weren't going to make it now either. We were glad you were trying again and hoping for you. But it looked hopeless. Even when one or the other of you talked to us, as little as you said, we could feel the intensity and frustration, in both of you. And your emotions hit hard right off the letter pages."

Fay pulled her car into the driveway of a brick suburban house.

"This is my mother's," she said. "We'll finish about Monica later." She looked at me and smiled broadly. "Get ready to be charmed."

I welcomed the distraction.

****

"I've heard so much about you, Dutch," Fay's mother greeted from the entrance of her house before she led us into the living room. "Come on in. Make yourself at home."

"Nice house," I complimented.

"My husband is a rather successful salesman. Industrial. We got this when Fay was a baby. It was a new development area at the time. Up and coming. We're happy. A good place to raise a family."

Fay nodded agreement.

"Just what did you hear about me, ma'am?" I asked while showing mock concern that she perhaps was referring to some illusory scandal as I sat myself next to Fay on the couch. I then looked toward Fay to finish the show and began to mumble just loud enough for Fay's mom to detect.

"You didn't say anything about the drive to the lake, right?" I asked Fay while feigning embarrassment. "You told me you would never let that out."

Fay burst out in laughter, realizing it was a made-up scandal I alluded to. Her mom studied us to see what she was missing in the conversation.

"Of course I didn't, silly," Fay replied to go along with my fake scene. "But now that you've let the cat out of the bag…"

Fay then looked at her mother grimly.

"Mother," she began, "this is the guy who knocked me up just before I left Frankfurt. Just after I broke things off with Joe. Actually, come to think of it, it was just before."

Fay's mother countered with a sly smirk, as if she realized this was a joke.

"He totally took advantage of me, Mother. I know I was the one who broke things off with Joe, but you know how it was between us. Four years together and it's hard to get your bearings when you know the relationship is over. Dutch pretended he wanted to comfort me while Joe and I were having our problems. So Dutch got me drunk and pounced. I mean pounced. I wasn't even that drunk yet. He was all over me."

A half-smile eased onto her mother's face. Obviously, probably, this indeed was a joke.

"When Daddy wakes up," Fay continued, "I want him to shoot him. I promised Dutch sex to get him to San Diego. Now we need to shoot him."

"Fay has a sense of humor," her mother said with a grin. "I'm sure you missed it these last two years apart." She then looked straight-faced at Fay. "Besides, your father is passed out drunk again."

Fay and I exaggerated our laughter at her mom's joke to lighten things up further.

"I will know to never set myself up around Fay again," I said. "Especially around her mother, who obviously taught her well."

"I had a fun upbringing," Fay replied.

"So, if we're going to be serious now," Fay's mother continued, "how long are you going to stay in San Diego? Are you returning to Texas from here?"

"I'm not sure what I'm going to do," I answered. "I just ended it with this girl from Los Angeles. Fay probably mentioned Monica. I'm still in a maze right now. It's perfect Fay is here to visit. She's exactly the one to help settle me. She's so empathetic, for one thing, but also she was our best friend there in Frankfurt. So it all kind of fits for me to visit her now."

"Well, I'm glad that worked out for you, Dutch. Yes, I can see how Fay can help right now. Do you have any plans for what's next for you?"

"Vaguely," I answered. "Just kind of want to get away somewhere. No commitments yet. Let the dust settle and get some direction."

"You don't have a job waiting on you in Texas, then?" Fay's mother asked further.

"No, but I need a job. Not just for the money. Something routine to settle me."

"That sounds normal. Yes, you don't want to just sit around. Things fester. Fay said you were in Houston until you came here to see Monica this spring. Is that where you'll go back to? Can you get your old job again?"

"Yes, I was in Houston until I left for L.A. a couple of months ago. But I hated it in Houston. And I hated my job there, too. Worst experience of my life. I'm not trying to sound negative, but I'm a country boy. I grew up on a cotton farm, went to a rural school, then went to a rural-oriented university—agriculture, engineering, oil, military. After I was in the Marines, I travelled in Europe, where I ended up meeting Fay, you know. Houston's a great city. It doesn't deserve my bad mouth. Everybody but me wants to live there. It's the fastest growing city in America, and booming. Not just oil money anymore, either, not to mention the second largest port in America, and the space program and all. Computer-oriented companies are moving there and modernizing it. I just didn't fit. It wasn't just my rural background. All these new families moving in, seeking a new identity. Money's great, but I didn't want to buy anything. I missed the old Texas. I missed studying, travel, even meeting people like Fay."

Both Fay and her mother smiled warmly with that.

"So where will you go next, then?" Fay's mother asked yet again. "After you leave San Diego? Where will you go if not Houston?"

"I was thinking of working on an offshore oil rig out in the middle of the Gulf of Mexico," I answered. "The money's good, and like I say, I don't have anything against money. I worked in computers, programming, in Houston. I wouldn't be making that kind of money on an oil rig. Not without a special skill anyway. I'll just be an entry level roughneck or something on an oil rig. You work like a week or two on and a week or two off. You get paid for twenty-four hours a day while on the rig. Time and a half after forty hours. So the money is decent even without a special skill, and there's no place to spend it. It's something I can quit easily, so no real obligation. That sounds good to me right now. That should settle me after a while."

Fay blurted laughter to share with her mother.

"I told you, Mom, Dutch is so Texan. *So* Texan. I mean, this guy is out of a movie."

She then looked at me, beaming approval.

"You are not like the rest of your generation," Fay's mother said with a smile. "More like from mine."

"He's from the South, Mother," Fay emphasized. "You've been in California too long."

"Do you have any other skills besides computers?" Fay's mother asked. "Since you don't seem so happy with that. A few months on an oil rig could change your outlook there anyway, you know. Computers might start appealing after a few months stuck with menial work in the middle of the ocean."

"I mean for it to change my outlook," I replied. "We'll see. What I really want to do after that is go to Nashville. I have a sister living there. Or near there, anyway. I'll spend my time off the rig there with her. I want to check the place out. I've always wanted to be a

93

Country singer."

"Yes," Fay swooned. "Yes. You do that, Dutch." Fay turned toward her mother. "You should hear him sing, Mom. You won't believe this guy. We all, me and Joe and Dutch and Monica, went over to this woman Eva's house all the time. She was always inviting us over for supper and to visit. And these two cornpones, meaning Eva and Dutch, Eva's husband too, would play Country music by the hour. And Dutch bought this beat-up, I mean corroded, if that's the word, guitar to learn how to play. Because he told us all, and by God meant it, he wanted to be a Country singer someday." She looked at me again. "Do you still have that old thing?" she asked me.

"My guitar?" I asked her.

Fay nodded yes.

"I left it at my mom's," I replied.

"You didn't bring it? I'd love you to sing to Mother. And me again."

"I bought a new one in Houston."

"So you found something to buy after all," Fay's mother said with a grin.

"Yeah," I answered awkwardly. "Yeah, ha."

"Where is it?" Fay asked me. "Your new guitar."

"With my stuff at your place."

"I didn't see a guitar."

"I stuffed everything over in a corner in the living room like you said," I answered.

"I must have been changing," Fay answered. "I didn't see all the things you brought from your car."

Fay looked at her mother to explain, "Since I only have one bedroom, he'll have to take the couch. I just had him place his things in the corner out of the way until then." She then turned back to me. "So, you can't sing to my mother. You stinker. You are singing to me tonight, though. If not tonight, then tomorrow. Before you leave, for sure."

She turned back toward her mother. "I remember when Dutch brought up wanting to be a singer at Eva's that night. Eva teased him. Everybody wants to be a star, you know, and Eva is this feet-on-the-ground country girl Southerner. She's heard it all before, you know. So she lets him know, yeah, yeah, sure. But Monica had heard him sing. I remember her telling me how when he was learning the guitar in their little studio apartment, how he'd sing these Country songs to her. She never dreamed in a million years she would love Country music. And then that night at Eva's, he sang this Hank Williams song. That's his hero. Hank Williams."

"He's my hero," I confirmed, "but the song I sang at Eva's was a more current song. By Tom T. Hall. He's the guy that wrote that Jeannie C. Riley song. She was his secretary in Nashville. That's why I want to go to Nashville in my off time from the oil rig. Just show up places in Nashville. Hang around. Find places that might help me out later on. Hang in there, you know. Anyway, Tom T. Hall wrote that song 'Harper Valley PTA' for his secretary. And the rest is history, as they say."

"Yes," Fay's mother said. "That was a crossover hit. Everyone knows that song."

"Hey, dude," Fay came in, "you did not sing any 'Harper Valley PTA' that night at Eva's. Or ever, as a matter of fact."

"But I sang another of his, a pure Country one.

'The Year That Clayton Delaney Died.' "

"Oh, yeah." Fay's eyes lit up. "Oh, yeah. That was so much better than 'Harper Valley PTA' anyway. You know the line in it—I still remember it—that really grabbed hold of me in that Clayton Delaney song?"

She looked back at her mother to explain. "This song, Mom, is about this guitar picker from this hick town in the South. Everyone was poor there. I guess Tom T. Hall grew up in it. But it was the Bible Belt, you know. So Clayton Delaney was this poor country boy in this small poor Southern town. But his ticket out was he was the best guitar picker around. But then he died. We don't know why. Up and died. But here's the words I remember. That I relish. Something like how he got religion at the end, and Tom T. Hall was glad of it. That is so beautiful. So real. So Southern."

She looked back at me. "You used to sing us some Gospel songs, too." She exuded serious demeanor as she looked again at her mother with more explanation. "You'd ask him to sing a favorite song, and if it wasn't Hank Williams, it was Gospel."

"Those were everyday Country Gospel songs, Fay. Stuff I was raised on."

"They moved me, Dutch. Especially the way you sang them."

I nodded appreciation.

"Well, you're going to have to sing some of them before you leave," Fay's mother said.

Fay glanced at her watch.

"We gotta go, Mom," Fay informed. "When Daddy gets out of his stupor, tell him hello," she said with a wink.

"He's in Phoenix on business," Fay's mother said

to me with a smile. "You two don't want to stay for supper? I was getting ready to cook."

"I want to take him into San Diego to a restaurant. Just to do something, you know."

"I understand," her mother replied.

Just as we got up to leave, as if on cue, the doorbell rang.

"That's probably our neighbor," Fay's mother said. "He heard Fay had a guest."

Fay rushed to the door to check it out.

"Hey, babes," she said to a tall, freckled, redheaded guy in a white grease-stained T-shirt. "What you up to, dude?"

"Hey yourself, Fay. I heard your Texas guy is here. I wanted to show him something."

"We were just leaving," she replied. "Walk with us to the car. Was that your motorcycle I heard a minute ago?"

"For sure."

Fay turned and motioned me toward her.

"Our neighbor here wants to meet a real cowboy," she said with a laugh.

"Hey, man," the guy said as he brought forth his hand to shake mine. "I heard a real, actually it was stressed to me, an *authentic* Texan is visiting Fay here. I wanted to give you a chaw. I got no one to chew with here in San Diego. Some of the guys in construction, I guess. Anyway, you do chew tobacco, don't you?"

"Ha," I blurted out. "Yeah, now and then. Just for cultural mixing. I hope you don't use the really hard stuff. You know, plug tobacco."

"Naw," the guy said, to my relief. "Syrupy stuff."

"Yeah, I can handle that. I'm not hardcore into

tobacco. Just kind of fun now and then to feel macho with the guys."

Fay's friend pulled out a plastic pouch of chewing tobacco. He opened it and grabbed a pinch with his thumb and front two fingers, then stuffed it into his right cheek. He then offered the pouch to me and I did the same.

"Let me try some of that," Fay said, looking at me with a gameful grin. "Cowgirls back home chew this stuff with you, don't they, Dutch?"

I snickered and nodded that some of them did.

Fay grabbed a wad likewise and stuffed it into her right cheek. She bit down on it to squeeze some of the juice and waited to see what happened.

"Come on," the guy offered. "The real test, Fay, is to chew while you're riding my bike."

Fay smiled so broadly, a slime of tobacco juice rolled down her lower lip onto her chin.

"Look at you, Fay," the guy said. "You're acclimating already. Let's ride my hog."

Fay followed him to his motorcycle, let him kick-start it, then crawled onto the back. She wrapped her arms around his chest as they rode off. A couple of minutes later, they were back, with a sour look on her face.

"Ready to puke it, Dutch," she said to me, looking down toward the ground. "How can you stand this stuff?"

"You ain't a real cowgirl unless we kiss," I teased.

She looked at me as if barely able to hold her stomach contents any longer.

"I'm not puking because of you, Dutch." Her look grew more nauseous. "People kiss with this stuff in

Texas?"

I stood expressionless.

She walked over to me, grimaced, then laid a tobacco-wet kiss right on my lips, even adding some tongue for encore. I was ready to gag, myself, but wasn't going to let it show. The guy that started all this watched, enjoying the show.

"You're authentic, all right," he said in praise of me. "How long you staying? Let's get together again."

"You want to join us for a bite at a restaurant?" Fay asked him.

"Naw," he replied. "Dutch just arrived. You two go on and relive old times. I just got off work anyway and don't want to stay out late."

"You got a job finally?" Fay celebrated. "Great. Where at?"

"I'm a laborer on a construction crew. Minimum wage. I almost didn't take it. That's highway robbery. I wanted six bucks an hour. These pirates."

"My first job was at a cotton gin for less than minimum wage and no time and a half."

"And you took it?"

"Hundred-hour weeks. Saving for college. Now I have skills. I make more than six bucks an hour."

The guy checked me out as if I were being a smart ass. I was. I was disgusted by California even more now.

Fay frowned at me to get me to back off.

"We should go, Dutch," she said as she dug deep into her cheek with her forefinger to shovel out the nauseating wad of chewing tobacco. It seemed like long minutes while she was digging, spitting, and gagging to get the chaw out of her violated mouth.

"Nice to have met you," I told the guy.

He shook my hand but still seemed to think me a smart ass.

Fay waited until we got to the freeway before she lectured me about her friend.

"He's a nice guy," I told her in response, "but this is why this country is going to hell. He's the pirate if he thinks unskilled entry-level work is worth even minimum wages. No wonder no one wanted to go to the war. Nothing to do with politics as much as the feeling of 'Now we're all victims. Life shouldn't be so hard. So challenging. So complex. Only easy answers.' "

Fay looked at me with a pathetic expression that eased into a smile. She reached over to hold my hand.

"I love Texas, Dutch. I'm so glad you're here."

She kept hold of my hand the entire drive. I could feel my hormones bubbling.

****

"San Diego is a pretty town," I said to Fay as we walked into her house after our evening at the restaurant and then driving around. "I have a lot of affection for it, too. And I'm even part of the census here, you know."

She looked at me while pondering what I said.

"Would you like a last-minute refreshment? A glass of wine, or a beer, or maybe a soda pop or something?" she asked me after we sat next to one another on her couch.

I shook my head no.

"So we have something else in common besides Frankfurt," she chirped. "We're San Diegoans. I guess the correct term is San Diegans. I'm not really sure. So does that make us kin somehow? How were you part of our census?"

"I entered Marine Corps boot camp here in February of 1970. One of the first things one of our processors told us right off the bat was how we would be a part of the San Diego census, since that was a census-taking year. I have to admit, I was bugged. I didn't mind San Diego so much, but the thought of being part of California for the 1970s population irked me to death."

She let out a laugh at my expense.

"Do you really hate California that much?"

I nodded yes defiantly.

"My God, why, Dutch? I know there's a rivalry and all, but you take it so seriously."

"The rivalry is probably what got me started. But Texas is so looked down on by y'all. By most, but by y'all for sure."

"I don't think so. Texas has a lot of respect. A lot of movies about Texas. And Texans."

"Yeah, but y'all think us goons."

"That's true with some. But that's just regional bias stuff. Don't take things so seriously."

"My parents grew up in the Dust Bowl, the Woody Guthrie era and demographics. As a matter of fact, he spent a lot of his Dust Bowl days in the Texas panhandle. So did my parents. They lived like that. Thing is, I'm not ashamed of it. I am so proud, and not just of them but to be a part of that culture through them. This is the America I love. Not the poverty-stricken one but the survivor one. The can-do one. The overcome-adversity one. We came, we saw, and we the hell conquered. Adversity. My mother later on graduated with a master's degree in History. She made

Who's Who in America. My dad quit school after the eighth grade, the first year he could quit. I doubt he wanted to continue anyway, but it was to help out on their farm. And hiring out to other farms, too. They were sharecroppers, farming twenty acres until depleting it, then giving it up, twenty acres somewhere else until depleting it, but all at the same time hiring themselves out to other farmers too, just to stay alive. But my daddy was smart and ambitious, and when World War II broke out, he lied about his education. I guess they didn't check all the new recruits with the war that just started, and he said he had a high school education. That was the minimum to be eligible for Officer Candidate's School. The ninety-day wonders. He did well on his tests and became a lieutenant in the Army Air Corps and the pilot of a B24 bomber. He was an ace pilot and won the Distinguished Flying Cross. Came home with G.I. money and bought a farm with water and fertile soil. I'm so proud. I'm not a goon. I want to bite some of these pricks here in the throat if I even think they think so."

She blurted out laughter again.

"Oh, my dear Dutch," she howled. "You are a card. I can assure you no one ever could think that of you. You toy with people with your intellect and all you know. Ease up, dude."

"I met some from California in the Marines that let me know otherwise, Fay. I'd hear stories about all the Okies that moved here during the Depression, meaning not just from Oklahoma but any Southern country-bumpkin type. And they did not say that with respect and affection. They thought we were all monkeys. I hated their guts for it."

"Well, I'm sorry to hear this, Dutch. I know people can be that way. I'm sure it did happen to you. And down South you have your attitudes about minority groups. It's life. I'm not excusing it. But don't let it get to you so much."

"I could take being an Okie type. Yes, I'd get angry, but I know who I am, as they say. What I really resent, and I mean resent, huge, is how people flocked here, not just from the Dust Bowl, but after World War II, like this was the Garden of Eden, and then their kids grew up, our generation, I mean, spoiled brats. Don't know the meaning of hard work, duty, or anything else that their parents had accomplished to get California so well off. Why sacrifice? Suckers do that. Party, surf, smoke dope. Okies can do the work."

"I know why you're saying all this, Dutch, and there is some truth to it, but you're being a bit harsh. There's a lot of good Californians our age who do know the value of hard work and patriotism and duty."

I nodded agreement.

"I also knew a lot of those types from California in the Marines," I confirmed. "It's so easy to simplify and exaggerate, I know. I shouldn't get so carried away with the bad I've seen. But it scares me. We're losing something here. No good is going to come out of the party mindset we're developing, even in Texas, except we're blessed enough to be goons more."

"You were this way in Frankfurt," Fay commented. "You didn't really say all that much, but you said some pretty appropriate things sometimes. I got the gist of it. You hated Joe. And it helped ruin you with Monica."

"Joe was a phony anyway, Fay. I ain't picking on your boyfriend, but he was so phony. Monica thought so too."

"You both were glad I broke it off with him." She sighed. "I'm aware."

"I know you got together with him in high school, and we can all be naïve in high school, but you stayed with him for four years. Nobody could figure out why. I was almost shocked you broke it off with him, except it was perfect that you did. Yes. Finally."

'You're hurting me, Dutch. I saw things in Joe you didn't. That's all I can say."

"I can go with that," I said as apologetically as I could manage.

"Let's get on another subject. We've had such a good time together, but now we've gotten on how California and my California boyfriend suck..."

I grimaced and looked away, embarrassed.

"How much of Europe did you see?" she asked, giving the conversation a new direction.

"All over," I replied. "How about you? After you didn't have that VW van of Joe's to travel around in."

"I saw quite a bit. Since we worked for the Department of Defense while on that base, we got treated as tourists by Europe, and not residents. Legal status, I mean. Meaning we were treated as if we came from America, rather than residing in Europe."

"Yes, I know. I used that status too, to get a Eurorail pass."

"Yes, that's what I was leading into," Fay said with fervor. "Before I left Frankfurt, I got a Eurorail pass. First-class travel on any train in any country except England, Greece, and the Eastern Bloc—the Common Market countries, in other words—for twenty days. It was wonderful. You could even sleep on the train. I did that several times. I felt I was wasting the pass if I wasn't on the train all the time."

"Yeah, me too." I chuckled at the memory. "And since it was first class, we not only got luxury travel, but most people couldn't afford it, so a lot of the time you could get a whole compartment to yourself. At night you could spread your sleeping bag out and sleep."

"Problem with that, you're on the train asleep at night, travelling, rather than getting to see the countryside, or stopping now and then at a place."

"Double-edged swords to everything," I said, shaking my head at the irony. "For sure we had to be selective when to get off the train and stay some place. Anyway, where all did you go? Your choice spots."

"I never made it to England or Scandinavia. But I really wanted to see Amsterdam."

"For the prostitutes?" I joked.

"Ha. But I did want to check out if they served a joint at hostels, like I heard."

"They did," I iterated.

"You checked that out?"

I nodded yes.

"I thought you were down on drugs."

"I am. The whole mindset. But you and I indulged at my apartment with Monica and Joe sometimes. I know you remember that, so what's the question for?"

"We got you high for the first time," she said with a smirk. "I couldn't believe I'd met a guy who had never been high from weed. But you're from Texas, so I let that explain it."

"You had to blow the smoke deep into my mouth to get me high. I was just being sociable the few times I shared a joint with y'all. Once Joe's hash gave me a headache, but I still didn't get high."

"So I decided, by God, I know how to get you high, and I did. But you scared us. We thought you were going to work us over. You looked so serious, even malevolent."

"So much for peace, love, and dope, huh." I snickered as I thought back to the incident. "It was the only time in my life I ever got high. Overrated. All this talk about how mellow and deep we are on a marijuana high. I believe you, but I had heard occasionally about reefer madness, too. But even now it's how love and weed will save the world and they are kissing cousins. So I was surprised to feel so on edge, and I had to concentrate to not make a ruckus."

"Well, you scared us, all right. If Monica hadn't been there, I would have kissed you and massaged you to mellow you. Instead, I just told you to stay in bed and do your best to control yourself. As I recall, we never smoked again the whole time."

"I don't know if I was disoriented and distrustful or what. But I did not feel mellow and wanting to save the world. That I know. For whatever reason, it came out that way. Anyway, I did take a couple of puffs with freaks while I was hitchhiking around Europe, to make them feel as one with the universe or whatever. But I haven't even considered smoking since then and probably never will again."

"I don't smoke anymore either, and you and I for sure won't smoke together," Fay said emphatically.

"Anyway," I said, going back to the previous subject, "when I was in Amsterdam I decided to indulge in a joint at a hostel, just for the times. Indeed, they gave one with breakfast, just like I had heard. Weed is not a hard drug, and if I don't indulge, or much, it shouldn't hurt me too much. It's what's going on, and I don't live in a cave, so I did it also. I guess the word is 'experimented.' Hard drugs are addictive, and that's a different story. But yeah, I wanted to check Amsterdam out for that too. The joint at breakfast. Just to see. Anyway, Fay, where else did you go?"

"Of course Rome. And Paris. All over France, actually. Really loved France. And Spain. Loved the Mediterranean all over. All the Rivieras—Spanish, French, and Italian. Next thing I knew, my twenty days were up. I timed my last day for Luxembourg, to take Icelandic Airways to New York. Then on to home."

"What was your favorite place?"

"Avignon, I think," she said, thinking back. "The French countryside is so wonderful. The people in the rural areas are so friendly. Unlike Paris. I almost hated Paris except for the sites themselves, like the Eiffel Tower and all. The people are so rude."

"Yeah, I know. I hated them. But the city and the sights of Paris were exciting, like you say. I loved the Rivieras too."

"So, Dutch, where was your favorite place? Holland, ha?"

"England. I did that outside of the Eurorail, of course. I stayed an extra month or so after my Eurorail ran out."

"I so envy you. I should have travelled with you. I felt safe for the most part as a single girl on the Eurorail, but if I had gotten out, really out, I don't know what all might have happened. I know Europe is safe overall, but you never know what's going to happen."

"It's ironic how our supposed-to-be travel mates were gone by the time we travelled. Then we were on our own anyway. I'd have loved to travel with you too, Fay. You would have been fun. Plus you appreciate things."

"You're making me regret now, Dutch. So what would we have done if we had travelled together? Since we both did Eurorail but then I went home, what did I miss?"

"Whereas you timed your twentieth day to get to Luxembourg to fly out, I timed mine for Brindisi, Italy. That's on the Adriatic coast. From there, I caught a boat to Greece. If you go to Athens, you get a free stop at the Greek Island of Korfu on the way. I met a girl there on the boat, as a matter of fact."

"What's this met-a-girl stuff? I thought you and I were travelling together now. Did you just dump me? But seriously, Dutch, I'm not trying to make you feel guilty, but I knew Monica, and I'm kind of jealous for her. Weren't you supposed to meet Monica when you went back to the States? Men are such scum, Dutch. Damn you."

"Wasn't quite like that, Fay. I did meet a girl, but let me finish the story before you slit my throat. And about Monica, I'd already determined that if I did meet a girl, scum that men are, I would indulge. I was very aware the odds of Monica and me making it were slim, and here I was in Europe, my one fling, perhaps, for doing this. So I'm supposed to vow celibacy because of a doomed future or something? I wasn't looking for romance at every port, I was just living day by day, but I wasn't going to turn anything away. If a girl made me forget about Monica, then I should know. If it helped give me perspective about her, then great too."

"Aw, that's what they all say."

"Whoever 'they' is, then they are right. No matter what it sounds like to you, I wasn't trying to have my cake and eat it too. I was at a turning point in my life, and I was in an exotic setting, and I wanted to live it."

"I can see your point, Dutch. Actually, I would have done the same thing. If I was going to look Joe up when I got back to see if we could make it or not, I'd want some European experiences to arm myself with. To comfort myself with, too."

"Good. Thanks."

"So what about this girl?"

"This is why I love to travel. Not just travel, but live, and beyond the routine of things. There wasn't anything special about her. I don't want to make a big deal out of it. But she was special in her own way—a quiet way, you might say. God, I love life, thinking back about it. How there's all this out there in life. To stumble across or to study or blend with. No expectations. No judgments. Just experiences."

"You should be a writer, Dutch. That's what a writer would say. Okay. Get to this girl. My side is hurting now, anticipating. Anticipating what, I don't know."

"So," I continued, "I was looking over the side of the boat, taking in the Mediterranean. We had just passed Albania. I saw Albania across the waves in the distance. This radical Communist country. I've heard they get around by donkey carts. No idea. But there was Albania, and I felt special just to be looking at it from a boat. Two girls came along after a while and started staring out too. Just travelling you get in receptive moods, and suddenly these two girls and I were talking. They were from Toronto. One was a brat and complained about everything—everything had to be set up just right or the whole trip was a hassle, et cetera. The other girl looked subdued. She wasn't all that pretty, and before you get on to me about being a shallow cad, I was glad she wasn't. It made her more special. It added to the stoic demeanor she had. She had a bearing about her, lived in her own ordained world. And was somehow now stuck with this brat of a friend she had."

"That was touching, the way you put it. More than touching. You added depth, an artistic depth, to the scene, talking about the girl."

I smiled, as much because of the connection Fay and I were making as for any flattery she was throwing my way.

"Finally, the brat went off to get coffee or something. The other girl moved closer, next to me. She asked where I was going, and of course it turned out we were both getting off at Korfu. But after that I was going on to Athens and then wherever in the Greek Isles. Just talking about all this made the girl swoon. She looked at me and all but invited me to spend the night with her on the beach at Korfu. She wanted to dump the brat so badly and be with somebody who slept on beaches and ventured off to new places. But reality hit, and she let me know how she felt responsible for her friend. Her friend was helpless, basically, and she had to take care of her. But the longing was so huge in her to spend the night at the beach with me in Korfu, and it made my juices churn. She knew she was dreaming, but maybe, just maybe her friend would agree to that. And would I put up with her friend, too, so this girl I was talking to at the time could have one night of a substantive memory of being with a guy on the beach in Greece? But her friend came back soon and the girl would have none of it. They were going to a hotel, and that was that. No sleeping on any stupid beach, Greece or no Greece. The stoic girl's disappointment was so pathetic. She got out her address book and got my address and gave me hers. Just in case someday we ever got the chance, you know. So nothing happened, but maybe you can figure out why I'm telling you the story. I felt like we'd had a fling, even though not even close."

"Yes, travel is not just places," Fay affirmed warmly. "This is the Dutch I remember, for sure. The social one. This is why you ended up helping so many people back in Frankfurt. Not just Monica, and me and Joe, but those hippies who were on their way to India. And that guy from New York, later on. We were all like stray puppies and drawn to this divining rod of a soul you have. People found you back in Frankfurt as if they sought you out."

I held back a blush at hearing myself described so by Fay.

"So what else did we, you and me, do as we travelled together back then?" Fay teased. "Take me with you some more."

"Greece was wonderful—not just the famous sites, and not just the history, even though those alone were great. I went out of my way for some other things, including hitchhiking down to Sparta. Sparta is sacred to me, especially in this Age of Aquarius my generation stuck me in. I didn't do anything there. I just wanted to be there, breathe the same air, sort of."

"You're such a romantic. I would have gone with you, though. Some of this would have rubbed off on me."

"What's special about Greece is not just the history. It's all these islands, too. They spread throughout the Mediterranean, all the way to Egypt and Turkey. You can bask in the sun there, if that's your bag, or just flavor things. It's a treat. I only did a couple of the outer islands, but I love Greece for that and for the food, the scenery, the history, the music."

"Did you do anything after Greece?"

"I hitched around for a couple of weeks, just for the lifestyle. Stick your thumb out and see where you end up. You meet all kinds of people, too, some of them strange. You get picked up with a sales pitch sometimes, both sexes."

"Just what do you mean by that?"

"What it sounds like. You better be ready. Some pick you up just to have a pickup. I had to be on my guard, and that's all I'll say about it. I was lucky. It was all easy to handle. I didn't particularly like guys hitting on me. I was polite, but no way. Most people don't want problems, just some fun. They'd back off if you let them know you weren't interested."

"Did any of the women entice you? You know, like to endeavor."

"Whole families would pick me up and take me to a villa with them. It's a tolerant age with a lot of people, and they are happy to share with a stranger. Some of them got off to me being an American."

"But the girls, Dutch. Tell me about any endeavors. You're ignoring me there. I don't mean to push, but are you afraid to tell me? I'm not even dying to know, but I do want to know. This is exciting, even charming. What all did I miss? I would love to just throw my fate to the wind like you did. So while we're travelling around together, share what we did. Get it?"

"Nothing exotic happened, and like I say, I wasn't necessarily looking for it. Especially with Monica hovering inside."

"But..."

"Yeah, there's some buts. Sort of. But don't get your hopes up."

"Okay, I get the gist. And if you don't want to talk about it, I'm okay."

"A few I'll mention, now that you brought it up, are like the girl on the boat to Korfu. Nothing happened. But still, part of me, just for the flavor, will remember them probably, at times, for the rest of my life. One was a redneck, though. Pothead redneck. A lot, male and female, would offer me a joint as soon as I got in the car, just assuming I was a hipster, short hair or not. I usually turned it down, not only not interested in drugs, even marijuana, but to broaden their horizons, too. You know, here's someone not into pot that just entered your life. I wanted them to know that not everyone cares about this stuff. But this one girl, the redneck, as soon as I turned down her joint—and I mean the very instant, because it was already lit and she was smoking on it—she slammed on the brakes and kicked me the hell out. To her I was either a blasphemer or maybe an undercover agent or something."

"Maybe she thought you were being rude. Mussing up the social decorum."

"Whatever. I got a kick out of that. But the other

memorable girls were so unique. One was a stoic type, just like the girl on the boat to Korfu. But the other one, I don't know. She only spoke French. I never knew what was going on. Very pretty. She picked me up in rural France, drove me all over the place. She knew I only spoke English, but she was going to share whatever world she needed to share anyway. She never asked me a question, that she made known to me as a question, anyway, just talked in French for miles. Like it was so important to tell me all of this. But she didn't seem crazy to me. It was a crazy scene in an eccentric way, but somehow there was logic to it. Then she pulls over to the side of the road, politely smiles, and lets me out. Not mad, not needy, not playing games. Just thanks for listening, and good luck."

"No punch line here, you're saying."

"I'll remember her, but not because it was eccentric or that I was thinking she had a deep desire and attraction for me. She seemed to really like me, but I don't know. I was afraid to get my hopes up that she was seducing me. Being a disgusting guy, I started hoping. It just didn't seem like she was needing me for that. But she was friendly. And the ride, her picking me up, seemed to be fun for her, not needing it to be fun for me. And I don't mean fun like having a blast. She seemed to really need to talk to me. Whether I understood a word or not. I let her fantasize I understood, because she knew I didn't know French. She just needed to share and pretend I understood, I guess, and I adored her for it."

Fay blurted out a chuckle. "That indeed was an art scene, Dutch. I mean a canvas painting of words. I wonder what it would look like in a watercolor. So, any other girl stories?"

"To me, this other stoic girl was even more endearing, if that's the word, than the Korfu girl. I was in Ireland, had just left New Ross, the ancestral home of John F. Kennedy, and was hitchhiking to the coast to take a ferry across the Irish Sea to Wales, then on to Luxembourg."

"The last stretch of your trip, in other words."

"Yeah. So on the boat I met this woman with her son. She looked to be about our age, in her twenties, I decided, maybe early thirties. She wasn't pretty, either—not ugly, but average looks. And a bit chubby, more like husky. She was a truck driver. That's how she supported herself and her son. We started talking and getting to know one another. She was such a serious person and wanted to understand things, their context and meaning. Her son was probably about eight and a chip off the old block. He also had a calm, serious demeanor and a need to study life as he lived it. The way he would add to what his mother said, or ask me a question in order to get me to delve more into a subject, he seemed like in his teens with his intellect. That alone moved me. The two of them, with nothing special in their environment or setting, had a depth to them. And me being American, soon I attracted political attention. There's a Communist movement over there. Some guy on the boat worked at a canning factory started by Trotsky-Leninist investors. I admired that. They put their money where their mouth was. But this guy was so into Communism and bragging about this factory, how just and egalitarian it all was, unlike us greedies in America. But then this woman truck driver challenged him. She seemed defensive for me, and I liked that. It was as if we had a rapport, but also she was very knowledgeable and somehow it increased our rapport. She let this guy know how the factory was doomed to fail, and it did, very soon after that conversation. I read about it after I got home. She countered him with why Communism had too much idealism to work in a practical way, with its ideals of folly. And this failure to recognize reality is what made it so ruthless in trying to get it to work, she explained to him. She showed disgust, too, not just philosophically but that he probably just became a Communist recently and that's why he was so gung-ho for it. And that was the case. He admitted it."

"She was worldly wise."

"Yeah. So much. Maybe more than anyone I ever met. And again, that just made her looks all the more appealing. Her physical looks were just her book cover. She had all this rich literature inside of her. She lived in Cornwall, and Cornwall is a place I always wanted to see. When we docked in Wales, she had these trucker plates that let other truckers know she was one of them. Truckers stop to give each other rides and all. She invited me along. Invited me to stay with her in Cornwall a few days."

"Please tell me you did."

"The idea really appealed to me. I adored this girl. But a few miles inside of Wales, a guy stopped that was going all the way to London. I took the ride and left her. I saw the look of disappointment on her face. And that was my ending with her instead of getting to tell you about a marvelous weekend I spent in Cornwall with her and her kid. I will never forget her or forgive myself for not going with her."

Fay grabbed my hand as she shook her head in amazement at my stories.

"I never met anyone like you." She sighed. "I already knew that, but I'm still getting to know it. Instead of girl stories of frolic, you have ones out of a page of Dickens or something. I love that, Dutch. And it fits you more than I already knew but I guess could sense. You were the most caring and kindhearted person in Frankfurt. Not just to me but to everyone I saw you with. And it comes so natural to you. This Southern hospitality or whatever it is."

She looked at me seriously for a moment, thoughts on her mind, studying aspects of me, perhaps. She then tilted her head slightly and looked me straight in the eyes.

"Listen," she said just above a whisper. "It's late. You're not sleeping on the couch." She let that sink in to me, then leaned over to kiss me on the lips. "Let's go to bed now, Dutch, and all that it implies. It's been a while since I've had a man. I've fantasized about you, knowing you were on the way here. And now here you are. Let's make up for lost time. Beginning right now."

****

I could not remember the last time I'd slept so peacefully as that first night with Fay in San Diego. And peaceful was the perfect word to use. Natural, blissful peace.

How had something like Fay never happened to me before? I didn't have to go back in time and relate every happiness I ever had, or every sexual encounter with a girl, be it erotic, flirtatious, meaningful, or heartfelt. I'd never experienced anyone like her, ever. She entered my life, created a rapport, oozed affection, and shared with me, in the most alluring and casual manner, a freshness and fulfillment she seemed to take for granted in her life. Life was so natural with her. So common. But somehow so special.

I felt the bed from her side indent slightly next to me as the sun began to shine through the edges of the window inside her bedroom the next morning. I opened my eyes and saw her watching me with her smile. I loved her naked form. I had a sheet covering the lower part of my body. I wanted to be naked with her. Again. So I kicked the sheet off me.

"Would you like to shower now, Dutch?" she asked. "I thought about showering with you after we made love last night, but I left it open because we might just make love again. Then we fell asleep. It felt good just to cling and linger after sex. I hated to lose the essence."

She began to rub the bridge of my nose with a fingertip.

"It was wonderful with you, Dutch, by the way, in case your ego needs to hear this stuff. It's been so long with me, and I missed it." She smiled again with a tease. "I'm not trying to make you feel like an object, but you were that too, if you don't mind. But it was wonderful. Someone from my past, that I am close to, that I desire. I'm not a prude, I have no qualms per se with sex just for sex, but somehow I don't really get into just the sexual thing. That has its moments, but it feels so empty so quickly. It gets so out of hand. I needed you for the emotion part, too. Used you twice. In stereo."

She gave yet another teasing smile my way before she lay with her chin on my chest. I maneuvered my arm around her shoulders as best I could, trying not to disturb the tranquility I hoped she was feeling while lying with me. I then pushed my hand onto her breast to stroke.

"There, Dutch." She sighed. "That's it. That's the place. We're going to make love again, aren't we?"

She brought her head up to look at me. Excitement was on her face. She then moved her hand downward to further excite me.

Pleasing each other continued to entice us, the need to fulfill a partner while being the object of glorifying desire. We needed more than sexual symmetry. There was something sacred about making up for our lost years. The cheated years. The ones spent somewhere oblivious instead of together.

"Are we going to be able to get out of bed today?" Fay asked me friskily, while kissing me over my lips and neck.

Kissing Fay. I was kissing Fay. I loved kissing Fay.

"I have to use the restroom," I answered bluntly, making a face to show I felt guilty. "Does that put a muck on it for you enough to kick me out of bed?"

"Ha. Yes. But so do I. Back to earth, right? But then we can shower together. Then start again with sex."

She was gorgeous while I stared at her as the perfect last sight before I jumped out of bed for nature's call.

"I'll follow you," she said while getting up. "I'll run the hot water in the shower while you're doing your thing. You have a nice ass, by the way. And your washboard stomach still turns me on."

I wanted to flatter her in return, but it felt corny. So

I hugged her quickly before continuing on to the bathroom.

****

Happy.

I felt so incredibly happy. I could not remember the last time anything was like this.

"What do you want to do today?" Fay asked me over coffee at a late breakfast. "And to let you know, we don't have to rush things today. No need to do everything in one day. I'll miss work tomorrow. I haven't used any vacation time yet this year."

I shrugged my shoulders and began to think about where to go.

"I assume you want to go to the Marine Base," she suggested.

"We can't get on base. And even if we could, I'd want to go where they live and train in boot camp. We couldn't do that, no matter what. But it would be nice to drive by, at least, to recharge the memories."

"The Navy-Marine base is off Barnett Avenue," Fay informed me. "Where else would you like to go today?"

"Actually, I've heard for years about the best zoo in the world being in San Diego."

"That would take several hours, but we could do it."

"That's plenty, then. We already had a beer on the beach last night before we came home. I do love the beach, and you have islands just offshore. But I'm fine. I don't need anything more, for now."

"We could go to Coronado Island and bask around tomorrow. Can you stay another day? You don't have a set schedule, right?"

"No. I'm in no real hurry. And I'm here with you. Why rush?"

She smiled and nodded her head.

****

Somehow, San Diego was in one part of my demographics brain, as was Camp Pendleton, while California was another entity in another part of it. I felt good in San Diego. And now it was Fay's town to me, also.

"Look," I said pointing toward the Marine recruit drill field as we drove along in Fay's car later. "You can see them. Their trousers aren't bloused, so it means they're in phase one."

"What are you talking about?" Fay asked while trying to share my excitement. "Phase one—you mean like the first stage of boot camp for incoming Marine recruits?"

"Yeah. The extreme first stage is just showing up. You arrive at the San Diego airport before midnight and wait around at parade rest until the rest of your platoon arrives."

"What's parade rest? I've heard some of this stuff from movies or people talking. I know it's some kind of stance a military guy does."

"It's a rigid version of relaxing in military formation. So you come from wherever with a full head of hair and civilian naïveté. You report to the Marine Corps area at the airport for guys ready to go through boot camp. You stand there at parade rest so it starts sinking in you're in the Marines now. Then you wait until the last recruits show up from other planes just before midnight. You already are under the command of these guys wearing the Campaign hats, or Smokey

121

the Bear covers, as they call them. These guys already seem to hate you for being stupid. When I arrived from San Antonio, where I was inducted, it may have been the peak of the anti-war movement, or close enough. There were a bunch of hippie types near the Marine reception area at the airport. I already knew what was going to happen to us in training and how we were going to be treated like we were guilty of stupidity, then get manhandled in training no matter what we did. So I got to thinking, while we were at parade rest at the airport, just what is the Marine Corps going to do to me that they weren't already going to do to me?"

"What are you talking about? They hadn't done anything to you yet, except make you stand there and hate you for being stupid."

"But they were going to do things. Horrible little things. So standing there in formation and being treated like an amoeba just reinforced to me what was ready to happen to us real soon. And watching these hippies a few yards away, who were mocking us by saluting us and marching around in fun, I decided I was going to do something about it. What were these Marine sergeants going to do to me about it that they weren't already going to do anyway? If not these particular guys, other Marines, the drill instructors in boot camp. It's all a part of training, to straighten us out and toughen us up. So I figured I might as well start now."

"So, my dear," Fay said with a smirk, "just what the hell did you do that night at the airport here?"

"I didn't ask permission. I just broke ranks. This sergeant was going berserk and screaming at me while he tried to catch up with me. But by the time he got to me, I was already in the hippie area. The hippies were just looking at me, wondering what I was up to. I walked up to the first one I saw and punched him in the face. I got swarmed by these hippies, but the other Marine sergeant came over by then, too. The hippies hadn't hit me yet, but they had surrounded me and were angry and screaming at me and threatening me, nonviolent that they were. Ha. The Marine sergeants were apologizing to them and let them know what was going to happen to me and to please let them handle me. So the hippies backed off."

Fay blurted out in laughter.

"I can almost see you doing that, Dutch. Is that true? Did you do that?"

I smirked and nodded yes.

"I could only assume the Marine sergeants thought I was cool, I didn't really know, but their job was order. One of them grabbed me by the throat and screamed at me how I better fall in line, lecturing me that Marines are fighters but they aren't thugs, et cetera. It was a good speech. Then the sergeants lectured all of us about discipline and the harm that vigilantes and mobs do. A life lesson, you might say. Then we all had to do fifty pushups right there because of me. One of the sergeants took my name down."

Fay was beaming in humored radiance while bobbing her head, thinking about my story.

"So what happened to you?" she asked.

"Nothing besides getting choked, screamed at, and made to do pushups. Anyway, while still in this initial stage, the pre-processing stage, you get your head shaved, you mail all your civilian clothes home, take your first shower to get all the civilian off you, and then stay up all night and clean, clean, clean. You get a

physical exam, a dental, and then take tests to
determine your IQ and your strengths, and all that.
Nothing was said about the incident I created. Once
they've got you processed, you meet your drill
instructors to begin phase one, the initial training stage.
Phase two is the rifle range at Camp Pendleton. And
phase three is the final training stage after you return to
the Marine Corps Recruit Depot here in San Diego
from Camp Pendleton. Phase three is the last mopping-
up stage, to get all the training and discipline nailed
down."

"MCRD, you mean," Fay said to show she knew
the base name where we trained.

I nodded yes.

"We knew we were pretty slick by phase three," I
continued. "Ready to be full-fledged Marines. We got
to have our trousers bloused to just above our boot tops
with an elastic blousing garter. That's the sign you are a
hoss. Not a Marine yet, but beyond a maggot. That's
how I knew those privates we saw just now were in
phase one. By the time you're out on the drill field like
we just saw now, but your trousers are still unbloused,
you're finished with processing and move on to your
platoon area and get assigned to Quonset huts, one
squad per hut. You get your rifle and uniforms and so
on. I almost had a college degree and did well on my
tests, so got offered some choices like intel and stuff. I
turned all that down. I wanted a rifle, a bayonet, and a
hill to charge."

"Wait a minute. You had a college degree already
and weren't an officer?"

"I was just short of a college degree, actually, but
still eligible for Officer Candidate School. I was set to

be a Marine officer out of college. I was in a program for that anyway, but my senior year I read where Nixon was going to pull the Marines out of Vietnam. I finished that semester, even had my college ring, but then enlisted as a private in the Marines, hoping I might still get sent before they started pulling the Marines out."

"I never met anyone like you, Dutch. I mean never. You are your own man. You see things like other people or not, but you see things like you see them. End of story. I don't know enough about the war to know if we belonged or not. I heard stuff and read some things and that's all anybody ever talked about, but I never really got it. And it seemed to me, in all the shouting at one another, nobody else ever really got it either. I didn't know what to think. One side said one thing and then the other side hated everyone's guts for thinking something differently. Being a girl, I wasn't going to get drafted, and I sure wasn't going to enlist. So I just took all the arguments in and let it slide. I didn't and still don't know who was telling the truth. Or who was lying the most, maybe. Anyway, it wasn't that I didn't care about the war. I just didn't know who was right or why."

"At least you saw it as complex, Fay. Everybody else in our generation knows we're imperialist pigs. So that's something else I like about you."

She looked over at me and winked. "So finish your story, Dutch. Now you're in boot camp, this first phase."

"Yeah. In the beginning, the first month, you are the slimiest of the slimes, and you don't get to blouse your trousers."

"Here we go again. What the hell is that?"

"Your fatigue trousers are left straight down, like I said, like normal trousers that civilian slime wear. You're a dork, a nerd, a puke. And it's drill, drill, drill, physical exercise, cleaning, cleaning, cleaning. Even a lot of classrooms. So, we got to our Quonset huts and were assigned to squads. My senior drill instructor loved me to death. He was a black belt in karate, with two tours of combat in Vietnam. You had to be a combat vet to be a DI. And he loved my gritty attitude. Figured out that this guy, me, came to fight. And he saw on my record where someone put how I punched that hippie in the mouth at the airport. I was his man. So it worked out."

"You have so many stories, Dutch. You are so interesting." She looked at me for emphasis. "You are so much fun."

So was she, but I was going to tell her at a time that didn't sound like just repeating a compliment.

****

I felt badly about dragging Fay to the zoo. She was my host and seemed to enjoy the role, but zoos are something you take for granted if you live near one. Surely, this had to bore her. Except with Fay, everything was a go. I wondered if she ever got bored doing anything. So as much as I enjoyed zoos, I went out of my way to enjoy her zoo with her. It was fun to be happy openly with her.

"Let's have a cocktail at home tonight," Fay said at the small Italian restaurant we chose for our evening meal. "I have wine. Cowboys drink wine, right?"

I nodded yes.

"And then an encore performance in bed," she said

with a seductive smile. "Too bad we can't bottle sex and have it with our wine at lonely moments."

I nodded my head in amusement.

"Are you tired?" she asked. "You haven't spoken much since we arrived at the restaurant."

"I'm not tired, but I am winding down. I enjoyed it. I love it here, I think."

"Even though it's California?"

"Maybe I'm making peace with things. Though I've always liked San Diego anyway."

"Making peace is good. And it's really good having you here, too. I was so looking forward to you showing up, but this is the first time we've gotten to be us as us, for me to be one on one with you. It's worked even better than I envisioned."

"Peace is easy with you, isn't it, Fay?"

"Yes, it is. But what kind of question is that? Do I seem naïve to you? Some people these days think if you don't know struggle, you're naïve."

"Yeah, you're right about that. People easily assume you can't be happy unless you're in an unchallenging environment. But everything seems easy with you. It did in Frankfurt, too, but here I am on your turf, and you're the same happy, caring person."

"My life is complex enough. I don't go out of my way to muddy any waters. There are people that annoy me sometimes, but usually there is something to like about someone. Things to appreciate. Minimize the negative in my life and I'm still challenged. Life flows better when I flow with it. I wouldn't want to sell out some value system or anything. There's plenty to fight about. But I prefer flowing."

"You put it so simply, and you make it work for

you so simply, but actually, no one does that. Flow with the flow. No one. But you do."

She smiled appreciation at me.

"You know what Monica said about you?" I asked her.

"Am I going to like it? She seemed to like me. I guess I can take some criticism if what you are going to tell me is negative. And she is one who thinks happy people are naïve."

"People so down on everything, like Monica is," I explained, "like to think of themselves as deep and insightful. Only their astute awareness can appreciate the full extent of how badly the world sucks, you know. And only their untiring fortitude could endure such a plight as that heavy knowledge."

"She was deep, Dutch. You've said as much."

"Yes, she was, but simple enough to settle for hate. She couldn't see two sides to anything without one side being evil somehow. She never got past that. So she wasn't that deep. She and her ilk have to assume somehow that happy people like you can't know anything. Or can't take the brunt of the suckingness of life. Otherwise you couldn't possibly be so happy, so flowing."

"She told you I was shallow?"

"She liked you too much to say that about you. I was glad she liked you so much, because I did not want to hear you run down like she did everyone else. But you are the type she would say something like that about. You know, being shallow and that's why you're happy. In your case, she respected you too much. It's like you passed her test. But I wondered if she thought it, at least some.

"Anyway, once in Frankfurt, and then again while I was in L.A., she brought you up to me. About us. Us, meaning you and me together. She told me both times I should go after you. In Frankfurt it was when you broke things off with Joe. She was bugged with me anyway because of how aloof I was toward her by then.

"But again, just now in L.A., she told me I should go after you. That you'd be good for me. Maybe that was half insult, too. I really don't know why she brought it up. But there I was, given permission. It was obvious she and I weren't cut out for one another, and maybe she was giving her blessing, or maybe I couldn't handle someone so in depth as her and belonged with the frivolous happy creatures. I don't know. Except she liked you so much. Respect liked, not just friends liked.

"So I took it as we had her blessing, that we seemed natural together. She said all this in a sincere, reserved way. You just never know with her ilk, but it made me think there was something obvious about us, even though you and I never flirted with each other. Was she jealous at the thought, or was it an obvious thing to her about us somehow, and deserving of her approval?"

"I'm going to take it as her blessing, Dutch. I'm not just trying to put a good spin on things amongst friends. She did show me a lot of respect. So maybe in the crevices, in her value system, like you say, some of this negative in her was linked to the idea that happy people are airheads. But I think she loved and respected us both, and she probably meant it sincerely, maybe even jealously, that we belonged together."

"I thought so myself, actually. I told how already I had felt an attraction to you. You're so easy to like, to adore. You're so pretty and so much fun, so caring. It's easy to be attracted to you. But I was so in love with her, and you with Joe. I could never take any attraction about you seriously. Until now."

"Until now?"

"You know what I'm talking about. Seeing you now is wonderful. For its own self, not just because of memories, but because it is."

"You want that wine?" she asked. "I'm ready. Let's go home. I feel a conversation coming on. We can relax better at my place. Just wine and conversation."

"And sex."

"And wonderful sex."

It was just our second night together. The freshness and excitement was still there, but somehow, now, it also seemed commonplace, that we were in our groove.

****

"Would you consider staying?" Fay asked me at a seafood restaurant on Coronado Island the next day.

"I told you so last night," I replied. "That I hate to leave. If there was any way to stay…"

"Yeah, but that was in the simmering process after making love. Men are always agreeable after sex. You didn't sound convincing."

"Yeah. I'm not convinced. But not because of you. I just left Houston. I told you how miserable I was there. What would I do here? Look for a computer job? You can't just take a job like that and quit the next day. What if I'm miserable here? In spite of you, that is."

"Can't you sugarcoat this a bit, Dutch? I know what you're trying to tell me. I think so, anyway. You can't trust your happiness here even if we're happy. But it's kind of biting at me, like I'm not good enough to make you happy here, or not good enough, period."

"I know. Sorry. Just trying to be honest for both our sakes. Thinking out loud. Truth is, I can't stand the thought of leaving you. And San Diego isn't Houston. And I don't have anything staring me in the face saying, 'Come get me.' There's no Bali Hai out there calling me."

"What about being a Country singer?" she asked. "I thought that was staring at you now. How much does that mean to you? Don't you want to go for it, the dream?"

"It's a big enough dream. But it's only glamorous if you make it big. Otherwise, it's one gig after another. Or no gig at all. I just love the music and sharing it. And the thought of making it big, with people wanting me and my songs.

"But there is a 'but' now to that. I'm scared now to leave here. I've never been this happy so easily, and it's because of you...and we haven't even fallen in love yet. I'm happy just from the rapport, the fun, and the compatibility of being around you. I can talk to you about anything. Or nothing. I'm happy from not feeling like we have to talk. Or that we have to do something. It's all so natural and easy with you; you are so easy to get along with. So I can put off that dream about Country music."

"That was better, dude. A much better presentation to use on me. So it's like you might stay. We don't have a relationship yet. We haven't fallen in love yet. But I would hate for you to leave. My happy life would find ways to feel dissatisfied, now, if you leave. Suddenly my happiness hinges on you.

"I do hope you will stay. I'd love having you in my

life. But don't look for a computer job yet. Let's just live day to day. You could get a menial job. I have an apartment. When you find work, just help with the rent. We both have cars. We both pay our way. We don't have to do anything, like party or go places, so you don't need a fancy job. If it works out like we think it will, then you can get a computer job or whatever later, if it comes to that. If not, then be a Country singer if it still suits you."

"No pressure," I mused. "All the better about all this. There's no pressure. Day-to-day stuff together. Happy until we're not." I looked at her and nodded with emphasis. "What's left to think about, then?" I asked.

"So we're a go?" she asked with a smile.

"Yeah. Yeah, we are. We're a damn go. Yeah. I love that. Fay and Dutch. A pair. There goes Fay and Dutch. They're together. They're a pair. They look so good together."

"So what's going to be our song?" she asked. "Since we're not in love yet, it doesn't have to be a big dramatic song. But we should have a song, don't you think?"

"Sure, you bet. We rate a song. We're a pair. That rates a song."

"I've got one, unless you think of one."

"Go ahead. What?"

"We're both Beatles fans," she said. "How about 'Why Don't We Do It in the Road'?"

"No way." I laughed. "But for now, why not? When we fall in love, then something better. Kiss on it?"

"Okay, but no tongue," she teased. "We're in public."

"I read a statistic where relationships that start off living together," I said before I kissed her in celebration, now feeling earnest, "that if they ever get married, it ends quickly."

Why was I thinking of a stat like that as Fay and I made our sudden plans together? Marriage didn't seem in the air. We were having too much fun for that. But that's what made the idea of marriage so appealing. I could do this for the rest of my life, it seemed to me, if I lived it day to day like this. To purposely not take it so seriously was only to relieve pressure that marriage might suddenly introduce itself. The fact was, I was very serious about Fay. It was just all happening so quickly. If I'd lived already in San Diego, there would be no need to move into her apartment. We could ride our happiness and let things happen. Instead, it was time for me to leave. Except I wanted to stay and Fay wanted me to stay. So I had to move in. Action. Already a statement of some sort. That was serious.

"Don't think about it, then," Fay said with a grimace. "Get this serious stuff out of your head, or we won't do anything in the road. Get it?"

"I've worked several menial jobs in my life," I mused out loud. "Construction, cotton gin, waiter, driving a delivery truck. The more menial the job, the more my stay in San Diego will seem a transition. A rebound. A rebound not just from my relationship with Monica but also from my life in Houston. I haven't been happy for years now. Now it's dawned on me how emphatically I *am* happy, and I want to stay that way. Because of you. It's like some revelation. As if to say, 'Why have I not thought of this before?' More precisely, as if the genie of happiness is out of the bottle now and I dare not, or cannot, put it back in the bottle."

"Happiness is easy, Dutch. Problems happen, sometimes worse, but mostly happiness is so easy."

"That's why I'm here. I believe you. So now, that kiss to seal this…"

I followed the kiss by looking out at the majestic blue waves of the Pacific Ocean from our restaurant window. It was some kind of symbol for me and my new life. More feelings and memories were on their way now in my life. Right now. Right in front of me.

"You know, when I decided to leave Houston and go live with Monica in L.A., all these country-boy feelings came out of me. I was still very hesitant to see Monica. It was more hope than need, going to see her. That and knowing I got to leave Houston. But even then L.A. was no alternative, just thinking about it. So, to live with myself, I guess, to ease the fears I had of more Houston ahead in my life out in L.A. with Monica, I pictured leaving Texas on a horse. Leaving my car at my parents' house and just getting on a horse and riding across the Western states to Monica's house."

"And sleeping under cactus every night?" she blurted. "I know you were a Marine and bivouacked, or whatever you do, but wouldn't sleeping on a blanket on the ground for weeks get old? It's a fantasy, but still, the hot open sun during the day and then the cold hard ground at night would spoil any feeling of freedom to my fantasy. Freedom isn't free, as they say."

"I never owned a bed my whole time in Houston," I replied. "I felt claustrophobic as soon as I moved there and never bought a bed. A mattress seemed too permanent to me. I couldn't live with any feeling of permanency. I placed a Mexican serape on the floor in my bedroom, and that was my mattress."

"I guess you're already beyond that with me. You seem to enjoy my bed."

"That's why happiness took me so by surprise since I've been with you, Fay. But Houston was an easy act for you to follow. That's why, all the more, we've got to be sure about us. Anything post-Houston, post-Monica, was a step up for me. We need to go slowly and live day by day like we're doing, until we fully trust this is about you and not just improvement."

"Got it. Let's see how happy you are, first. Before we get too serious. Maybe anything looks good to you from where you've been. I'm game with that."

****

The next day I found work at the first place I looked, a large department store that needed someone to help deliver furniture and appliances. I had a job and it started immediately. On the spot. That meant that staying with Fay was official now—another step on the happiness road.

"So how was your first day on the job?" Fay asked me that night as we ate our first evening meal at her apartment as a couple.

"I've done this stuff before. I'm big, and I don't mind heavy lifting. Most of the day is standing around or riding in a truck. Good to be home, though. How's your day?"

"It's routine to me. It's very repetitive work, being a keypunch operator. But I've learned the little secrets and can crank out the keypunch cards. The computer world is quickly changing, though, with smaller-sized computers storing and cranking out more volumes of data. I'm expendable. I don't know how long I've got in the computer world, but real soon I'll be outdated, unnecessary. I'm glad I have secretarial skills. I've thought of becoming a legal secretary someday. Maybe I should make the switch soon. Maybe I can find a law office that needs secretarial services, too, as well as a keypunch operator, and get my foot in the door while I can. You know what I've just read, speaking of being expendable…"

I looked at her in curiosity, waiting for her to explain.

"I read about this just today, as a matter of fact," she mused. "It was an article on the back pages of the newspaper. There were these college guys from Stanford who invented a computer small enough to place on top of a desk. I kid you not. It doesn't do all that much, but they've already got buyers for it. They incorporated just this past April. So. Ha." She snapped her fingers symbolically. "Just like that, everything's changed," she said, shaking her head in disbelief while waiting for me to react and share her concern.

I stared back instead, waiting for her to go wherever it was she was going with all this.

"One actually invented the machine in his garage," she continued. "One was a gee-whiz marketing guy. Anyway, they formed a corporation, like I said. It takes three to form a corporation, so somehow there is another guy involved, too, and so they are a company now. I can't imagine how a computer that small can do anything worthwhile for a business, but on the other hand, most businesses don't own their own computers. They hire time from computer-oriented companies. So, what that means is that this little clunker of a machine might be improved soon and businesses will start using them instead of subcontracting their needs to specialized computer data companies—meaning this little computer might take off, and I doubt it uses punch cards for its data input. Just something to think about."

"So you're saying if you had just gone to Stanford?"

"Ha, ha. And you? What have you invented lately?"

"So you're in some kind of transition yourself," I commented.

"Aren't we always? I don't know how long either one of us will feel snug."

"Well, we're snug for now, and that's what all this is about. A lot of great stuff transitioning us right now, not just unsureness."

She stared at me as if pondering something. She then nodded her head and leaned over toward me.

"That rates another kiss, then, doesn't it?" she said just before laying a soft wet one on my lips. "We're in this together now. Facing the odds. Let's go and tell my mom. I'm excited about us."

I had no idea how her mom would handle my moving in. But Fay had been with Joe forever before I came along, so I figured her mom was already acclimated by now to this kind of arrangement.

****

"Well, it's a welcome surprise to have you back with us, Dutch," Fay's mother said as we all sat in the living room of her home.

"And this time Daddy is here," Fay added.

"I hear you're a good shot," I said, straight-faced, causing Fay and her mother to chuckle.

"Where did you hear that?" Fay's father asked.

He was a short, balding, pot-bellied man with a serious demeanor. I was glad Fay took after her mother in physical attraction as well as personality.

"We were talking about the war when Fay introduced Dutch the first time, while you were in Phoenix," Fay's mother said, to continue the joke.

"I was a non-combatant in World War II," Fay's father explained. "I was in the Navy in the Pacific. We were never fired on by the Japanese."

"We got onto all kinds of conversation last time," Fay commented.

"So I don't fully understand the situation," Fay's mother said to change the subject, "but I hope things work out for you two. Can you survive on minimum wages, though, Dutch?"

"I have a bit saved from my time in Houston, and while I was in L.A. I worked for IBM in Thousand Oaks, in the transition of them moving their headquarters to San Jose. After helping Fay with the rent, I don't have a lot left over for the day to day and all, but I can make it, and if I have to I can dip into savings."

"Why would you want to work a menial job?" Fay's dad asked.

"Our relationship just sort of happened, Daddy," Fay explained. "It caught us both by surprise. There was affection and attraction going on in Frankfurt between us that we didn't have time for because of circumstances. Then when we saw each other again, it all came out. Maybe we were both looking for something, too. Anyway, we want to ride the waves for a bit and see if we're serious. Right now, it's so good to see these feelings, and we don't know how seriously to take them. So Dutch is delaying going back to Texas, just to see what's real about us. That's about the best I can explain it. He'll get a good job eventually, whether he stays here or goes back home or whatever happens."

Fay's father looked at me to see what I thought about all she said.

"Yes, sir," I replied. "I was on my way home, trying to figure out what to do next with my life. Between the memories Fay and I had of each other and now the rapport we have—yeah, it seemed a huge mistake not to check things out."

"Well, I hope things work out for you two," he replied. "I suppose you have a healthy attitude about it—hopeful, but not indulgent."

"Well, listen," Fay's mother interrupted. "This is a very charming city, Dutch. I don't know how much you've seen of San Diego, but be sure to take advantage and look around while you're here. I know your budget is limited, but walking around is free."

"Have you been to the Old City yet?" Fay's dad asked, to add to the topic.

"Not yet," Fay replied. "We're short on money, so we'll be homebodies a lot. But I should show him the Old City of San Diego, yes. Just going around in it is interesting."

"That's right," Fay's mother said enthusiastically. "And Point Loma. That is so gorgeous, by the bay, and as cheap as you want to make it."

"And we'll go to Balboa Park," Fay added excitedly. "We've been to the zoo in it already, but that took so long we didn't see anything else. There are so many things in Balboa Park to enjoy. You'll love it here, Dutch. You'll be proud to be part of our population census for this decade. Now you can earn it, not that going through boot camp didn't earn that for you already. Anyway, these places alone will break things up for us if we get too bogged down in the dailyness of home."

"I would like to see more of this town, Fay, and just bask by the beach some, too. But actually, I just like being with you. I'm not trying to be corny. Home will never be boring with you there. But to see San Diego, too, will make it all the better."

Fay looked at her parents as she eased into a proud grin. They smiled back at her as if to say this had all the right overtones.

"So, Mom, on that note, it's getting late. We both have to get up in the morning. We just wanted to hit you with the news about us and talk about it. Don't mean to rush off so."

"You're already sounding domesticated," Fay's father said with a chuckle.

Fay's mother got up and walked to the door ahead of us. But instead of opening the door for our departure, she picked up a letter on the table next to it. She smiled timidly at Fay, then nervously at me.

"You got this in the mail yesterday," she said to Fay as she handed her the letter. "It was another reason I wanted to see you. It's from Oregon." Fay's mother gave an awkward sigh, then shook her head as she forced a smile. "I know this is awkward timing, but it's probably nothing."

Fay inspected the address on the letter then glanced at me. She prepared to say something, but focused again on the letter before ripping it open. Then she began to read.

After just a few sentences her lips began to tremble. She stuffed the letter back into the envelope, gruffly kissed her mother on the cheek, then her father, before she brushed by me out the door toward her car.

I stared briefly at Fay's mother, showing my confusion and disgruntlement, then walked out the door toward the car. I made a point of walking at a normal pace, not wanting to give dignity to the drama just displayed by Fay.

I made my way into the passenger seat of her car and sat looking straight ahead, showing no emotion—or so I hoped was the case concerning my expression. Fay had pulled the letter out again and was reading it intensely, with no sign that I was in the car next to her.

It was one page long, this letter she was clutching, with nothing on the back side of it. Fay stuffed it back into the envelope, almost wadding it as she did so, then looked straight ahead except that her eyes were closed tightly. A small tear trickled from the far corner of her right eye where I could see it easily without looking directly at her.

After a few seconds of this, she again opened her eyes, took a deep breath, pursed her lips, and looked my direction.

"I don't know where to start, but I owe you an explanation," she began. "I don't deserve it, but please be patient with me right now. I have to be honest with all I'm feeling. I owe it to both of us, but I want to be sympathetic with you at the same time."

She sat as if waiting for me to say something.

"Somehow," I said coldly, "this is about Joe."

She nodded her head yes, slowly, deliberately.

"He's begging me back," she said. "He's been

dating a girl in Portland, but he misses me and wants me back before his relationship with her goes further. He said he can't get over me and now has to take his feelings for me seriously, because he can't get serious about her, with all he feels for me."

She looked at me as if hoping I understood this nonsense somehow.

I wanted to spit in disgust and hoped it showed. The human part of me considered caring about all the emotion going on around, but just the thought of that got me disgusted even more.

"So?" I gave a low disgruntled moan as I gazed out the window, away from her. I thought for more to say, but not one iota came to mind.

"What, Dutch?" she blurted out, almost as if trying to smile somehow.

Then I looked her square in the eyes with my disdain.

"God, this was stupid of me," she said as she finally eased into her smile. "So, there, I ruined everything. Do you have feelings left for Monica?" she asked bluntly. "I'm not trying to put this off on you. You know, distract from what you just saw out of me. Can you identify with any of this is what I'm saying?" She looked at me with pathetically caring eyes, then began shaking her head. "I really don't love Joe still."

She looked up at the car ceiling and let out a loud laugh, then looked back at me. "You believe that, don't you, ha?" She reached over to grab my hand. I watched her hand come my way and watched myself allow it. That in turn made me laugh.

"I really don't love Joe. I'm serious. God! I have to admit every emotion I ever had came gushing out. I thought we were pure past tense. But it was there as I read the letter. He loved me, he wanted me, and I had memories of us when I did love him. That's the best I can do, dude."

She waited on my reaction.

I squeezed her hand but turned my look to straight ahead out in the street once again. I bobbed my head and curled my lip. Still there were no words in me for her about this.

"Will you stay with me, Dutch? I don't want you to go. I'm sorry this will be hanging over our relationship." She nibbled on her lower lip for a second. I could see her out of the corner of my eye. "If we still have a relationship," she continued meekly.

I wanted to reassure her. That was progress on my part, I decided. But as I searched for how, I still was at a loss and thought it best to leave things for now.

She released my hand and turned the key in the ignition, let out a huff of air, and began to drive. She looked frustrated and nervous but still confident. Confident in what? I knew what. She was still confident about us. That we were still an us.

"I want you to stay, Dutch," she repeated as she drove. "And I mean it with everything in me. I don't deserve you to stay, but I want you to, so badly. Please let honesty be the best policy."

"Honesty *is* probably the best policy somehow," I said with a slight groan, "but it still sucks."

She nodded as if in agreement and then let out a laugh.

We both remained silent all the way to her apartment complex, where I walked next to her on the way to her apartment. As she opened the door to let us in, I wondered if I was going to stay the night or pack my bags.

"Please stay," she beckoned as she walked to her bedroom ahead of me.

Instead of following her, I lay on the couch, saying I needed to take a nap, hoping answers would be waiting on me when I woke up. But I never managed the luxury of that sleep. Fay never came out of her bedroom, as if letting me alone to work things out.

I heard music coming from her room, soft music from a stereo, or so I assumed, anyway, since I never heard a disc jockey say anything between songs.

Did I still have feelings for Monica? Fay had asked me, and I hadn't answered. Could I identify with her at all about Joe just now? But I didn't want to know if I could identify. It wasn't fair of her to ask that of me, I decided.

I was angry, and the anger wouldn't go away. But I worked enough of it out finally that I could feel how I wanted her. And how I wanted to stay. I was leery of her now, but there was too much I liked about her to want to leave.

The music stopped in her room. I heard muffled footsteps on her carpet, coming toward me.

"You deserve better than me, Dutch," she said just above a whisper as she stood over me. "But give me another chance. You don't have to just trust me, but I can promise you nothing like this will ever happen again. And if you ever get a letter from Monica like I did from Joe just now, I don't know if I could trust you if you reacted to that letter like I just did. But I want you to stay, for what it's worth. And I'm hoping you've seen enough good about me and us that you will stay and try more with me."

That was perfect, I thought to myself. Just what I would expect Fay to say about screwing something up like she did. She still knew how to flow.

I sat up and patted the couch next to where I sat. She sat next to me and waited for what I had in mind.

"I love that we can have problems," I began. "That you have flaws. You're perfect with your flaws." I looked at her quizzically. "You really are over Joe?"

She nodded yes.

"I want to stay," I said, looking straight ahead.

"Then do. Please do, Dutch. I'm not glad I acted so emotionally and stupidly in front of you. But yeah, problems happen. I feel good you are giving me another chance. I hope I do the same for you if you ever pull what I did."

I chuckled. That was perfect again. She was a perfectly flawed person.

I put my arm around her and kissed her softly on the lips.

"Let's go to bed then," she said as she got up from the couch. "No sex, though. Just lay with me in bed and let's ooze back into our oneness."

I got up and we walked to her bedroom.

"I'll never do this again, Dutch."

I gave her a reassuring nod. Suddenly, I was glad this had all happened.

****

"You look tuckered," Fay said, looking at me sympathetically one evening as I stretched out on her couch and laid my head on her lap. It was shortly after supper, and we were watching a movie on TV.

"I don't know if it's nervous energy or what," I

explained apologetically. "I was this way on the farm growing up...and at the cotton gin, especially. We'd work hundred-hour weeks, sometimes, and I assumed it was natural to be tired. But some of my cohorts at the gin would go out on the town after a long day. I just have to relax when I get home, for some reason."

"Take a nap if you have to. I'm okay. I wanted to share this movie with you, though."

"I'm sorry. I don't do this often."

"You've been here two weeks now. This is the first time you've crashed early." She stroked my cheek affectionately. "It's nice, taking care of you. But are we going to make love tonight?"

"Just a quick nap, Fay. I'll be great. We didn't even move much furniture today. I don't know what's happened, why I'm so tired. A power nap and I'll be fine."

"What's a power nap?"

"In the middle of the day, when you have time to take a break, sometimes just a five-minute nap refreshes you."

"We have different metabolisms," she said with a laugh. "Take your nap."

As promised, I needed only a few minutes of sleep and was refreshed. I had seen the movie before and picked up points in it after I sat back up, to make her feel I hadn't missed anything.

"You're going to get bored pretty soon, Dutch," Fay said to me that night just before we drifted off to sleep.

I turned over on my side to face her.

"How did you decide that?" I asked.

"We never do anything. Every day's the same for

the past couple of weeks. We've only been to the beach once. We still haven't made it to Balboa Park. Not counting the zoo."

I smiled at her, teasing her worried mind.

"I must be the one boring you," I countered, "because I love coming home every day to you from work. And I love sleeping in late with you on weekends. You're fun to be with. Just being with you."

"How am I fun, dude? I want to believe that. But we do the same things all the time—have dinner and watch TV. And that's if you're not reading some book."

"We go to restaurants sometimes. I like your restaurants. Fay, we're living the day-to-day. That's what life's about. The day-to-day existence. And the ones I spend with you resonate. Are you bored? I guess I didn't think to ask."

"No, I'm not. We're even still getting to know each other. Not just filling-in-the-years stuff but habits and quirks. Moods. I just worry. I'm enjoying life together too. I just get scared you're going to tire of things and start wanting to go back to Texas, and maybe blaming me for things not turning out as well as you hoped."

I pondered for a moment, wondering if maybe she was projecting any of her own boredom on me. Or was she really worried I might get bored and felt vulnerable about it?

"Okay, we'll go out more," I replied. "I do like San Diego. I'd love to see more of it."

"You always say that, but then we stay home."

"That settles it. We'll go out more, and this time I mean it. But it's the going with you to wherever that's the appeal."

She smiled broadly and tapped my lips with her

fingertip.

"Just remember this conversation, Dutch. If you start getting bored and thinking our life is too normal, give me a chance, okay? I want to make you happy."

"I am happy. I don't need anything besides you to be that way. I grew up on a farm. I didn't go out much, growing up or in college. I take this all for granted. But I can see I'm not being fair to you. I'm glad you told me all this. We'll really go out more now."

"Are you in love with me, then, Dutch? I'm just asking, not prodding."

I nodded yes.

She smiled yet again.

"Then why haven't you ever said so?"

"Because every time I fall for a girl I tell her, and the next thing I know it's a disaster. So I'm not being superstitious, and I want you to know, but my feelings have always been there. And now that we're together, it's more defined, more obvious to me, but still the same feeling, the same emotion, as I've already felt."

"So you've been in love with me this whole time? You rascal."

"I may have been in love with you in Frankfurt even," I replied. "You always excited me and turned me on. I loved your personality and your flair, your common consideration for everyone. Your feminine mystique, as they say."

"I hope I didn't help break you and Monica up, then, if that's the case."

"You didn't," I assured her. "Except that I was so frustrated and depressed around her but refreshed again when I was around you."

"I still feel like the other woman, though." She

sighed.

"You sort of were. I wondered if it showed in me somehow that I liked you so much romantically, not just human to human. But most likely Monica saw the difference between you and her and felt inadequate. I don't know. It's all guesswork here about that. But I had a desire for you then, even though I wanted so much to work things out with Monica. I managed not to think about it, but it was there. I could control it, but it was there. I had to see things through with her, and I did love her. I still do. But I just can't stand her, too. Since you asked about me loving you, I told you how I loved Monica. Interesting angle, or what?"

Fay chuckled but quickly returned to her more serious demeanor.

"I won't have a bad conscience," she said, "but I don't feel good about it, either. We were all such good friends, and I loved both of you. You were both so good to us and good to each other, too, in front of us. I could see at times there were problems with you two, but Joe and I had our own problems. I must say that I liked what I saw when I was with you, too. But Joe and I went way back, and I had to be loyal to him. I know I broke things off with him just before Monica left, but it had nothing to do with you. Not directly. There were even things about you that sometimes got to me in a negative way. You take things in life so seriously. I'm a flow-with-the-blows type of person. But you had so much personality, and I loved your old-fashioned ways. So there was an attraction to you, too. It didn't interfere with Joe. I just had enough of Joe's negativity that I finally broke it off with him. It was more than negativity. I guess I don't have to explain. You and

Monica didn't like him."

"He was a phony. He tried so hard to have an ego but with no attributes to warrant it."

"There you go again, Dutch. I can't even mention his name without you tearing into him. Drop it. Yes, I broke up with him, and some of what you're saying about him was there and got to me. But you hit so hard with it about him. I know Monica felt the same way. But there was more to him than that. Anyway, I was ready to fly the nest. I was in Europe and wanted to spread my wings. So I did."

"So now that my secret's out," I said, to break the awkwardness, "do you love me?"

Her mischievous grin was seductive.

"Maybe," she replied with a giggle. She then rubbed my cheek nonchalantly to increase the tease. "I'm incredibly happy with you. I have feelings. But I'm enjoying this too much to start being serious. I like the pace we're going."

I showed some disgruntlement at her answer.

"Am I not being fair?" she asked, her grin remaining as she stroked my cheek all the more. "Does it create an imbalance inside you? And gives me some leverage over you, too? You poor thing."

"I don't want to push you," I replied, "or get you to say things you don't mean."

She leaned over to kiss me softly on the lips, then dropped her hand from my cheek to my neck, pulling me tightly toward her to kiss me more deeply.

"I absolutely love you, Dutch. So much. It's deep, and I'm so happy, enjoying it. I just didn't want to spoil what we've had. This day-to-day thing. It works its way in and gets serious as it does so. So I wanted to keep it light and happy. But I do feel a depth to it, with you. I absolutely love you. I can say it freely. And yes, it started also with me about you in Frankfurt…this manly guy with a heart of gold, helping all of us waywards as we struggled our way into your life."

She loved me. I remembered those cartoons I'd watch when I was growing up, how the young couple would kiss and fireworks would set off while sirens howled. I felt happy like that now. And somehow it didn't seem corny, even though it was supposed to be.

****

Our expression of love for each other seemed to start yet a new phase for us in our relationship. And with that new phase, as if to expand and to celebrate, we would share our surroundings more now, like I had promised.

"So, Dutch," Fay began just after we arrived at the entrance of Balboa Park, "what do you prefer? To walk around the trees and groves—you know, get back to nature a bit—or go to a museum? They have all kinds of museums here. We couldn't possibly cover them all in a day. There are several art museums, or one for anthropology, if you prefer, or natural history, a train one, or automotive, or science…" She looked at me to emphasize. "Or we could just walk until we find one we like. You're new here. You get to pick. Or like I say, we can walk among the trees and groves. It's part of an urban forest here, these groves and all."

"I love it here. I cannot believe I've been here in San Diego with you for nearly a month now and all I've done is go to the zoo and the beach. It is a great zoo, but look at this park! It is gorgeous. I am short of money and did want to adjust to you, so I guess I thought of

151

myself as a tourist if we went out much. Anyway, yeah, look at this place. We'll start doing some of this. Little by little."

"Yeah, great, dude, but here we are. So where do you want to start?"

"Let's just walk around. The trees and plants and all. That's free anyway. We'll take in a museum next time. See? I said next time. There will be a next time. I love San Diego. How's that? I'm part of the census here, so this is my town."

Fay smiled at me and placed her arm affectionately in mine.

Even the garden area was more than one could take in easily in an afternoon. That was good, however. It meant more visits and more walking around for free. I often had no idea what I was looking at, I just loved the landscape.

There was even a desert cactus garden. And something called an Alcazar garden that was small and easy to fit into our afternoon. It was not all about plants but was in the style of a Moorish garden and named after the Alcazar in southern Spain. It melded architecture, geometry, tiles, and landscaping into a unique, cohesive unit. It could have been displaying art for a garden to lure the imagination or epitomizing something of that part of the world—whichever, I didn't care; I just enjoyed it.

"It was great, Fay," I said yet again as we walked out to her car. "I can't wait to do this some more. And all we bought was a soft drink, besides our entry tickets. Next time let's splurge a little more, invest in our amusements a bit."

Fay nodded as she looked at me as if checking me

out. Perhaps she found amusement in my sudden willingness to spend some money.

****

I hoped I was not too happy now. I didn't have a guilt complex for so much happiness suddenly in my life, but it was disorienting. So much so there was a superstition about it inside, a feeling that if I thought much about it, the happiness just might go away.

"Are you asleep, my dear?" Fay asked me softly as she leaned over in the shadows of darkness in our bedroom to inspect my face.

"I'm trying to be," I answered.

"You're especially quiet for some reason. You're barely breathing. Is anything wrong?"

I shook my head no for an answer.

"Hey, you, talk to me, Dutch. I feel so alone right now. Warm me up."

"I feel so vulnerable all of a sudden."

"What do you mean vulnerable? Are you running out of money? I can reduce your rent. You don't have to pay half."

"Not vulnerable like that. That's why I'm for going out more now. We're making it with money, after all."

Fay waited for more answer, but I remained silent. She tugged on my shoulder for details of what concerned me. I turned toward her momentarily and looked her in the eyes.

"I love you, Fay."

"I love you too, Dutch."

I returned to my silence while turning back to my side. She sighed in frustration and tugged on my shoulder again.

"Dutch, help me out here."

"You don't get it," I said just above a whisper.

More silence.

"Don't get what, Dutch?" she finally asked. "Come on, turn around, quit being the martyr, or whatever it is you're doing. Talk to me. You feel vulnerable and you're in love with me. We've been officially in love for a couple of weeks now. It's been wonderful."

As I further lay quietly, she expressed her frustration more forcefully.

"I mean it, Dutch. Turn around and face me. Quit teasing me, or excluding me, or whatever this is. You're starting to piss me off. I'm your girl. We're together. Don't do this crap. It's childish."

I turned to face her but still didn't look directly into her eyes.

"That's what I mean. It's childish, Fay. I feel vulnerable and stupid and disoriented. I love you. I mean big. The real thing. Full throttle."

She almost smiled while she waited for more.

"I've been so happy…but like happy-go-lucky, like 'what a great period in my life.' But I'm hooked now. I love you completely. And I'm this little boy now. I feel at your mercy. You could hurt me so easily. And I mean *hurt* me. I can *feel* how you're able to hurt me."

She brushed her hand over my cheek, stroking it gently.

"Don't be scared of me, Dutch. I'll never hurt you. I'm in love with you too."

"Not like this," I replied.

"I don't want to compete with you. But you've opened up the floodgates in me. I have longing, an aching kind of longing. For you. My man. My total man."

I nodded acknowledgment of her feelings but lay still as I endured my persistent vulnerability.

"I was a mess when I first came here to see you. I was somewhat in turmoil much of the time in Frankfurt. I didn't know what to do with my life. It wasn't just Monica. But somehow you liked me anyway."

"Loved you, Dutch," she corrected firmly.

"I found favor with you even in a down period. That should be convincing to my confidence. It's comforting, but all of a sudden, I'm scared instead. Now we've come this far, and I can't live without it."

She reached over to hold my hand reassuringly.

"In the Alamo, they were all going to die," I moaned further. "But at least they had ammunition and cannons and long rifles and a fortress. They lasted thirteen days and took hundreds of Santa Anna's men with them."

She let out a laugh.

"You are so Texan. My God. You take it all. One minute we're deeply in love, and the next minute I'm hearing about the Alamo."

"I have no defenses for all I feel for you, Fay. That's what I'm saying. I'm scared to death. Just a total mush of feelings and fear of rejection."

She clutched my hand to her, and I became more calm.

"Are you at my mercy?" she said with a chuckle. "Putty in my mischievous hands? You poor thing, you."

I didn't respond to her tease, so she kissed me on an eyelid affectionately.

"You can trust me, Dutch. I'll love those fears of rejection away and full out of you. You are so precious. I can't believe how much. Total man and total love.

God, I hit the jackpot! I love you too, Dutch, so completely. There, it's out in the both of us. What now, my darling? What now, my total everything? We'll have to get a new song, for a start. We knew it would come to this. And now here we are. No crass fun Beatles song, but now gooey and deep. So what's it going to be, sweets? What's our new song?"

"How about 'Fascination,' " I answered without hesitation. "I can't get that song out of my head anymore. You know, that song by Jane Morgan, from the fifties, while we were growing up."

She bit her lip and giggled.

"Boy, you are in love, Dutch. That's the corniest song in history. I remember it. It was great when we were in elementary school and everyone watched cartoons."

"But it's our song now, Fay, and I love that it's corny. People will figure it out. If we ever bother to tell anybody. I don't care. That's how I feel. Floating and corny. In love with you."

I saw her nod affectionately.

"I love how you're corny," she said softly. "You're so real. That's what I like about you...love about you, too. You're so real. So much essence."

I squeezed her hand approvingly and felt emotional security flow back inside me.

"It's amazing how all laid out things can be in life," she said philosophically. "Our early years totally at the mercy of our parents for love, security, and structure. Then we branch out, form our own thoughts from all that and our experiences, and start making our own way. Then we're thrown into the arena of life. We have to make a living, go to war, gain a skill, have fun along the way, start finding out what life's really about and how our parents are only human after all. And then we fall in love."

She paused for emphasis. "And then we fall in love. Suddenly, that changes everything. Every last thing. I can't possibly consider life without you…without having kids by you…without sharing everything with you. With love and devotion as the glue."

"Does that mean we're going to get married, then?" I asked her.

"That's exactly and perfectly what it means. I only flirted with thoughts about marriage and family before. Happy little thoughts, often fulfilling. But now, this is what I grew up to be. With you."

I could feel my throat tighten at how much her words meant to me.

Nothing more was said for the rest of the evening. She snuggled next to me with her arm around my waist as we slept.

****

We were going to get married.

"Are we really going to do this, Dutch?" Fay asked me at supper the next day, looking serious and directly at me from across the table. "Now that we've slept on it, and gone to work and had time to adjust to it, are we really going to get married? Or was that just a spur-of-the-moment passion last night?"

She seemed nervous as she asked. That was a good sign, as if she was vulnerable, not pressured.

"It's what I want, anyway," I replied. "I'm serious. I really want it. But yeah, I've been going over it, the pros and the cons."

"The cons? So there are cons with you?"

"Of course. I know we're going to do it. I know it. I'm not letting you out of my life. But we've got things to work out."

"I know we do. That's always the case, but can I hear all you're thinking?"

"I'm here in San Diego, living with you, working minimum wage. Yes, I've got skills, and we'll do better than me working minimum wage. But I hated Houston. Not because it's a bad town—it's a great town. And even if I love San Diego, which I do, I could be miserable here. I'm sure married to you would work a lot out, with a great home life as a base. But I hated my job in Houston, not because of the company I worked for—they were great people, and yet it was a cold environment. I could tell myself that living with you, and loving San Diego, life would be different here and I'd be happy, but that's speculation. I don't know that. I was so miserable in Houston, and I have to take that seriously."

"So you're rejecting keeping your minimum wage job and living on love," she mocked.

"Fay, I'm going to marry you. You make all the difference in the world. So how are we gonna do this, ya know?"

"What about your dad and the farm in Texas?"

"I talked to him on the phone today, since you mentioned it. Times are hard, back home. It's already the poorest area in the United States. Not because of my father, but he's only a good farmer, not a rich landowner or a businessman. He said the hurricane there last week ruined most of the crops not already harvested. Last year it was a drought. We have irrigation, but when there is a drought, we have to compete for water. And inflation is bad now, and so are interest rates. So even with government subsidies, he's feeling the pinch. I guess it's good I didn't farm with him when I came home from Frankfurt, after all. He bought a bunch of new equipment for me, and I was going to custom harvest. He's doing that now on his own, to pay for the equipment. But other people are hurting, too, so there is less to harvest for others. He'll go to West Texas soon, and maybe they're okay there and he can pay for the equipment. But it sounds like he needs to live on what he makes from it to help pay for losses from the farm. I'd feel imposing, because there's hardly enough work for one, never mind two of us trying to earn a living there with that."

I saw the look of disappointment on her face before she eased into a smile.

"I was already daydreaming of living on a farm with you," she said. "Raising chickens and rabbits. Going to rodeos and all. Scratch all that, huh?"

"It's for the best," I replied. "But that makes it one less option for us."

"I like that you've been thinking about this. You're taking it seriously."

"I'm going to marry you, Fay. End of story. But I've got to think things through. The good and the bad. If I'm not happy in my environment, even being happy with you would be affected. So we're going to get married, and we have to decide just how do we do this."

"What about Nashville?" she asked.

"You mean my dream about Country music?"

"I could work while you sing in gigs or whatever happens. Maybe you'll get a song published. But I

159

could work. We wouldn't have much, but we don't now and we're happy. At least you'd be pursuing your dream in Nashville. Plus I don't want you having regrets about it because you married me."

"My sister just moved from Murfreesboro. That's the town near Nashville where she was living when I intended to go there. So we'd have to immediately find a place to live and find you a job. But that's a challenge more than a problem. Struggling toward a dream can be fun. But I don't know how much a dream all that is to me now, and not just because of you. Have you noticed I've been dragging my feet about it? I'm old school. Not just in my attitudes, but about the America I love. I don't really like all the Country music coming out these last few years. It's a big business, as they say. That's great. But the music and even the shows seem so canned, such factory-line products. I love the old cotton-fields-back-home stuff, and the folksy way it used to be played. It's all changed. America has changed, Texas has changed. I have too, but not like that. It just doesn't appeal to me anymore. As far as the dream part, were I to write a song that got published, I'd fly with it. But singing old songs in dives with a small audience that thinks me a square doesn't appeal. I'd rather marry you and settle down in every sense of the word."

"Okay, I'm listening. But the two biggest things in your life have been scratched off the list. Even living on love has been scratched off the list. Using the skills you've used before has been scratched off the list. We're out of options, Dutch."

"I've thought about going back to school. I have skills, but if I go back to get a master's degree, it may improve my options. You could work, plus I get the GI Bill, and I could probably be a grad assistant for some professor, too. I'd be making almost as much money doing that as I am now. Maybe more. A couple of years of that, and even if they don't need keypunch operators any longer, so what. You won't have to work then. I'd have a skill just in time to raise a family, so we wouldn't need your salary."

"Yes, we've talked about my options already. If I have to be a keypunch operator, I'll do it. But if I have to go off and get a new job like we've talked about, I'm going to use my secretarial skills. I would prefer it. So that's what I add to the mix."

She got up from the table and walked behind me to hug me while resting her chin on the top of my head.

"So let's do this, dude. We'll stay in San Diego, living on love, while you look for a school. Then you go on for a doctorate or get a job wherever, and we start raising a family. I'm snug again. Things never ever work out according to plan, but we have a nice plan, and let's believe in it and get some peaceful sleep in the meantime."

"Good. I love that too. And that frees us up to think we can marry and live happily ever after. Because that's what I want to do. Marry you. The sooner the better."

"You really mean this, don't you, Dutch?"

"I absolutely mean it. I have never been so happy or so confident."

"We're not going to have a big wedding, right? We can't afford it, and neither can our parents. Maybe mine can, but we're too old to think about big-wedding stuff and the-dad-foots-the-bill stuff. So do we go to Las Vegas and elope? Or Mexico's just a few miles away.

161

People elope there. Or how about a simple Justice of the Peace marriage and invite immediate family?"

"I'm for eloping, but I don't want to be rude to my family or yours. Let's bring it up to them and see what they say."

Our talk and our plans set me at enormous ease. And confidence. I had a life ahead of me that I wanted to live.

****

"My father," I said to Fay later that night as I put down the telephone, "wants us to wait to get married until after cotton season. Actually, cotton season goes all the way until November, or even into December if he's going to West Texas to harvest there by machine. Anyway, he was talking about late September, and maybe he could come with my mother to the wedding. He could get away for a day or two as he finishes up in south Texas and moves equipment farther up north."

"But school for you starts in mid-September," Fay replied, "if you want to get in-state tuition for California. You're too late if you wait that long to get married to me. It's almost too late now to apply."

"I already applied a couple of weeks ago."

"We hadn't talked about any of this then." She smirked. "You've been plotting all this for God knows how long. You sly little punk."

"It doesn't hurt to apply."

"My father is going soon to Saudi Arabia for a month," Fay mused out loud. "How inconvenient, I know. We're faced with being insensitive for the sake of saving a buck or two, aren't we? We need to get married quickly, so too bad for our parents. Is that what we're ready to do to them?"

"It's more than a buck or two savings, Fay. It's several thousand dollars of savings if I get in-state tuition here."

"You're going to use this as yet another excuse to go back to Texas, aren't you, stud? I can feel it coming. I know you. You're setting me up here."

"Not only would I get in-state tuition there, but I'd be going to a state flagship university that gets oil money from state lands to lower that tuition even further. We could probably get my master's degree for just a couple of thousand dollars or so, and I'm talking about for everything, not just tuition."

"But, counter, counter," Fay said with a laugh. "We've been through all this, Dutch. Keep making your sales pitch, but I have a job and a cheap apartment here. I could be looking for a better job as a legal secretary and all, but I do already have a job while I do that. I'd have to find one from scratch in Texas. So there. What if I can't, or what if it takes a while before I do? You're not going to win this, and you know it. Keep trying, if it makes you feel better, but I've got reality on my side. We have to get married either way. It just means we have to now, meaning in the next few days, if we stay here for your schooling. You just don't want to live in California. But again, as for the millionth time, you're already part of the San Diego census for 1970. And San Diego isn't part of California, even though it is, so quit worrying about being a Communist sellout in that regard. San Diego is a great town, and you love it yourself, you know you do. If you start your master's now, in 1976, we'll be out of here before the 1980 census anyway. So you're going to lose this argument completely. Are we going to get married now or not?

That's the question at hand."

"Are we going to elope or invite our mothers and settle for that?" I asked in frustration.

Fay thought for a moment and shrugged.

"I don't know what to do." She sighed. "We're the ones being selfish. I want to just do it and get it over with, and with both our fathers needing to be elsewhere, all the more reason. But it's going to hurt our mothers and make us look like inconsiderate brats."

"You're waiting for me to make the decision, aren't you?" I asked pointedly.

She didn't answer but continued her stare directly at me.

"Let's go to Las Vegas, then," I said. "We just have to spend a day there to register and go to one of those marriage drive-ins or whatever it is you do there."

She flinched and then nodded agreement with the plan. We kept our attention on each other, then eased into a smile. It felt good to know it was really going to happen, with the details finalized. We embraced and rubbed one another's backs, then kissed in celebration.

"Actually," she explained between kisses, "getting married in Vegas is easier than that."

"How do you know?" I quizzed her.

"Forget how I know. I assume you have your Texas driver's license. Bring it and leave the rest to me. I haven't gotten married there, if that's what you're curious about, but I know people who have, and Joe and I looked into it before we left for Europe, back in '74."

"No birth certificates?" I asked. "No proof that we're single?"

"None of the above. And we don't need blood tests, either. And no one-day residency requirement that you apparently heard rumor of somewhere. This is made in heaven."

"Heaven, huh?" I snickered. "Sounds more like this is why they call it Sin City."

"It gets more sinful than that in Vegas. This part is heaven. At least for us."

She kissed each of my eyelids, then clutched me tightly.

"We're really going to do this." She sighed. "You and I are getting married. It's like it was meant to be, somehow, even with Frankfurt as a part of it all. But I'm taken completely by surprise. Just, suddenly, there you are—ready to be my husband."

"Tomorrow is Thursday," I said, getting back to practical things. "Let's let our work places know, so they will be sympathetic enough to let us have Friday off without any more notice. Las Vegas is about six hours away by car—you told me that once, right?"

"Right at six hours," she confirmed. "Depending on stops and how fast we travel."

"We don't need a honeymoon, so we can be back at work by Monday. Balboa Park can be our honeymoon. We could drive to Vegas Thursday night, register at one of those quickie places, and get married by Saturday, then drive back Sunday. I've heard of things like this, anyway. Maybe all that is rumor, too. God, I didn't want a big fancy wedding, but this is pathetic. I feel cheap—except that I'm marrying you. That gets me by. That part is so special, but it still feels so cheap. And we're leaving our moms out, to boot. We're bad. We're so bad, Fay. I have a guilty conscience."

"We can divorce on Sunday before coming home,

if it makes you feel better," she said with a laugh, "speaking of Sin City." She then rubbed my cheek sympathetically. "Yes, Dutch, I know. But I know too that we're doing what we have to do. We want to marry, and it's best to marry here, or in our case, Las Vegas, in a wedding factory setting. And doing it expediently so you can go to school here more cheaply. But it lets me spend a couple more years in my hometown, too, before we traipse off to God-knows-where when you graduate. I don't mean for it to feel so cheap, and it does somehow to me too, even if we're doing what we feel we must. Even now, with rushing this, you can barely find a school before classes start. So we're going to do this and not worry." She kissed me in celebration yet again while grabbing me with both her hands behind my neck. "We're getting married. That's what I want. That's what you want, and that's what we're going to live…us being married. You and me. Man and wife."

****

The drive up to Las Vegas with Fay helped get me in the mood to accept our expedient version of a marriage. It was hot and searing across the Mojave Desert and Death Valley, though we had an air-conditioned car. The Grand Canyon wasn't far away, and I flirted with the idea of a honeymoon there, but we didn't have time for that. I loved the West, even the desert. I was set psychologically by the time we arrived.

I liked the entrepreneurial spirit of Las Vegas, and that's what I dwelled on, since I was stuck with it being the place where I got married. I was too much of a puritan somehow to like much else about it, glamorous city that it was. The rush-in and rush-out assembly-line feel of our marriage there didn't make me like the place any more from that puritanical aspect, either, appreciative as I was to have it available for our need.

We toyed with the idea of staying at one of the big casino hotels as a celebration, but we didn't have the money. Actually, I was glad we didn't. A poor, struggling marriage seemed more romantic to me. And the humble hotel we chose made me feel more down home.

We registered first thing in the morning on Friday and sought our time to do the vows. In the meantime, to Vegas it up a bit, we went into a fancy hotel to gamble. Our limit was five dollars each, just to be sure we didn't blow the money we didn't have. Frank Sinatra was in town, but his show was seventy-five dollars to see, so we said, "Forget that."

Speaking of assembly-line marriages, when we arrived at the chapel where we chose to marry, there was a waiting line, even though we had what we thought was an appointment. Maybe this would make us all the more determined to have a long, happy marriage, we decided. People were going to blame our decision to do things this way for any failure we might have in our marriage if we didn't make it work. That was something else to work on in our psyches as we awaited our turn.

"And you are the bride? Fay?" the man asked as he prepared us for our vows.

"Yes, I am Fay."

He then turned to me.

"Your name is Dutch? Is that your real name? Your legal name?"

I nodded that it was.

"It sounds like a nickname. But that's fine."

He was to the point but did bother with some endearments and counsel in the ceremony. I assumed he did that to make it feel like more than a legal contract. I was grateful, because I was determined to cherish everything. I was marrying Fay. I wanted to marry her. Nothing else mattered while I stood next to her, holding her hands as we listened.

But just before our vows, Fay began to giggle. I'm sure my fear showed on my face as she did so. A giggle wasn't harmless. Was she backing out?

"Are you okay, Fay?" the man conducting the ceremony asked, also concerned.

Fay blushed as she looked at me, then back at him.

"Everything is wonderful," she said. "I'm so sorry. I won't go into it except to say this…more to Dutch than to you…" She then looked directly at me. "You happened to be in California a couple of months ago, and I invited you for a weekend before you went back to Texas. You were my friend from our Frankfurt days. And here you are, two months later, in Las Vegas, with me, getting married. What the hell just happened?"

I began to chuckle also at the thought.

"Just a quick little rendezvous before we went on with the rest of our lives in the mundane," she continued, shaking her head as if in disbelief. "So tell me, Dutch, what the hell just happened? You know?"

She leaned over to kiss me gently on the lips, then winked in celebration.

This was the greatest wedding possible, I decided. I couldn't dream one up better than this. What a perfect way to start my life with Fay.

We turned back toward our bewildered host so he

could continue his duties for the ceremony. It was time for our vows.

"I now pronounce you man and wife," he said solemnly after the vows were complete.

Fay and I kissed, then held onto one another as we placed our foreheads together.

"My wonderful rendezvous with you, my darling wife," I said, beaming, "is only just beginning."

A word about the author...

A native of Harlingen, Texas, Larry Lee Farmer grew up on a cotton farm. He attended Texas A&M but dropped out to enlist in the United States Marine Corps, where he attained the rank of sergeant before being honorably discharged after three years. He worked as a computer programmer in Houston and as a civil servant for a US Air Force Base in Frankfurt, Germany, and traveled and worked in Europe for two years, which included flying to Israel in October 1973 to aid the Jewish State in the Yom Kippur War. He was also in Greece in the summer of 1974, when the war between Greece and Turkey erupted over Cyprus, and he was stuck on the Greek island of Ios for part of that war until he managed to catch a boat to Athens just in time to watch the Greek military dictatorship fold.

Back at Texas A&M, he finished his Bachelor's degree in Business Management and then returned to Europe and also Israel, where he lived for almost a year. Later he taught English and was a model in Taiwan, after which, while still in the Far East, he acted as a stand in and stuntman in the Hollywood movie *Inchon*, starring Sir Laurence Olivier. He then returned home to get a master's degree in agricultural economics at Texas A&M. With that in hand, he joined the US Peace Corps and served for three years in the Philippines. He also worked for several years as a computer programmer for the Swiss government. While in Switzerland, Larry was a country singer as well as a coach for the national championship American football team Bern Grizzlies. Since then he has been working in the IT department of Texas A&M. He has three children.

www.ingramcontent.com/pod-product-compliance
Lightning Source LLC
Chambersburg PA
CBHW072123170626
46813CB00004B/1665